MW01643926

Rumored Legacy

Rumored Legacy

A Dynasty of Friendship Series
Book 1

Molly G. Shane

iUniverse, Inc.
New York Bloomington

Rumored Legacy

A Dynasty of Friendship Series

Book 1

iUniverse books may be ordered through booksellers or by contacting:

iUniverse
1663 Liberty Drive
Bloomington, IN 47403
www.iuniverse.com
1-800-Authors (1-800-288-4677)

ISBN: 978-1-4401-0193-9 (pbk)
ISBN: 978-1-4401-0194-6 (ebk)

Printed in the United States of America

iUniverse rev. date: 11/12/08

"With humble heart and tongue, My God to thee I pray, O make me learn whilst I am young, How I may cleanse my way."

—A stanza of lyrics by John Fawcett. This is written on an 18th century sampler located inside Croft Castle in Herefordshire England.

Chapter 1

"Kelsey, tell me again why you needed me to come with you to this dress fitting?" Beth peered over her black framed glasses and contemplated her friend's request.

"You know how much I value your opinion. You just got accepted into the best fashion design school for a reason."

"I *can* solve just about any fashion dilemma." She looked Kelsey up and down. "Just how much leeway do we have here?" It irked her to see her best friend smothered in a solid peach evening gown. Kelsey's warm skin tone blended into the fabric with the appearance of a chameleon.

"I'm not sure. They have to clear every change with Her Majesty's designer."

"Why is the Queen suddenly taking an interest in you?"

"I have no idea. She is obviously informed what all her family members are doing, but it seems like this castle is very valuable to her. It is not even where the lineage began. Maybe she spent a lot of her childhood there and it's precious to her in that respect." Kelsey primped at her long, golden brown hair in the mirror.

"So what event is it this time?" Beth sat with her hands supporting her chin. Several tendrils of black curls bounced around her cheeky face.

"I think she's throwing a welcome gala for a Prime Minister from somewhere." They both giggled.

"Why do you have to go?"

"Even though I'm her Great Niece, she wants up to two hundred of her family members present so that it looks like we are all one big, happy bunch I guess."

"You'd better hide that bad girl image then!"

"Oh, stop." Kelsey blushed.

The Queen's dress fitter returned into the room. She took a step back and observed Kelsey standing in front of the three way mirror. "I think a sash of sorts might frill up the waist."

"Does she have to wear peach?" Beth exasperated.

The dress fitter glared at her without a word. "I will be right back with that matching sash, Kelsey." She walked out of the room.

"Are you able to bring a date to this thing?" Beth asked.

"I just broke up with your brother, Tim. I'm not that quick to get back out there! Besides, I don't know if true love exists anymore." Her electric blue eyes peered through her long bangs.

"Oh, the drama!" Beth put her pale hand to her head. Three silver rings adorned her fingers symbolizing the holy trinity.

"Shhhh. Do you hear that?" Kelsey asked.

"What?"

"The seamstresses in the back are talking about the rumors."

Beth noticed light whispers coming from the other side of the dressing room.

Kelsey motioned for Beth to come closer to the cracked door.

"The girl getting fitted out there is from the Royal Family." A seamstress gushed.

"I don't recognize her." The other employee whispered back.

"She's down the line quite a bit, but this may be the closest we come to royalty! There is a story that has been going around for centuries regarding her family."

"What is it?" The girl listened intently.

"Well, a long time ago, the King became very ill and had little in respect to male offspring. One of his sons followed his heart to the church, the other died in the war. Duke Rupert Dane was the King's nephew and only possible heir."

"What's so intriguing about that?"

"You haven't heard? Lord Dane's doctor declared him infertile."

A gasp came from the lady. "What happened?"

"A very ornate scheme began to brew." She paused for effect. "The Duke had two very intelligent, close friends, Testan and Wyn. One of them came up with the idea of having Dane adopt a baby and claim it as his own." Her voice escalated. "His so called marriage to Duchess Dane was so private that only the King and his two friends were said to be there. No one has ever seen a painting of her or had ever seen her in person. I believe it is part of this plot to pretend she gave birth to a child that was not of his Lineage." She sighed. "A report came out as soon as the child arrived, that the Duchess had died in child birth."

"Is that true?" The other woman questioned skeptically.

"No one knows since nothing can be proven!"

"Gosh, that would mean the Royal Family line would end!"

"Be quiet! I don't want any more mention of this. If they heard us, we'd be fired or worse!" The staff ended their conversation.

Foot steps clip clopped toward them. They both ran to their former positions. Kelsey looked back at Beth sitting on the settee and furrowed her brows with a sigh. She knew of these rumors swirling around the community.

"I apologize for the wait ladies, but the Queen found out you will be visiting Lord Dane's Castle tomorrow afternoon and asked I fit you for a day ensemble."

“I’m sure that isn’t necessary. I’m simply going along with Beth for a class tour.” Kelsey explained and turned to her friend. “Interestingly enough, I’ve never been there before.”

“Perfect timing.” Beth reacted having read Kelsey’s thoughts.

“The Queen specifically requested you look appropriate for your excursion.” The dress maker held up a pink tweed swatch near her bright blue eyes. “Lovely. I’ll have your suit ready for you to pick up by the morn’.” She clapped her hands twice and flicked her wrists. “Be off with ya.”

The girls waited until they had gotten into Kelsey’s convertible and were out of ear shot. The car’s brilliant shade of color conveniently matched her eyes. The gray leather interior felt cool against her skin.

She grabbed the padded wheel with clenched hands before starting the engine. It roared to life just as her emotions had from hearing the tale the seamstresses were gossiping about.

Beth attempted to break the tension. “Don’t fret over what those girls said. They don’t know what they’re talking about. Their lives are so dull; they had to make something up.”

“No. That is where you are wrong. I’ve heard it before. Mind you it was a while ago, but it has been going around for quite some time.”

“Does the Queen know?”

“I can’t be certain. I’m not close with her or her immediate family.” Kelsey turned the wheel. “No one would dare say anything in front of her.”

“She knew you were going to Lord Dane’s Castle tomorrow.” Beth smirked.

“All I could ever wish for is to have a family like yours.”

“What is so special about my family?” Beth brushed her hair behind her ears.

“No one is simply *informed*. You actually have conversations with each other.”

“The grass is always greener.” She said pointing out Kelsey’s vehicle and designer clothes.

"Beth, you tell me about your family reunions and after church dinners. They even come to your school functions. You have each other to lean on and go through the trials of life with. I have none of that."

Beth knew she felt very alone and looked away. She turned back towards her friend. "You've always got me."

Kelsey smiled and patted her on the hand. "I have to wonder if there is a way to figure out if the secrets are just a myth or the truth." Kelsey stared off into space.

"Now how on Earth would you be able to prove or disprove something like that?"

"I'm not sure, but if I could, wouldn't you think I'd get that conversation I've always wanted with Her Majesty? I don't want to be invited by obligation anymore. It would be nice to have real relationships with all of them and not just because they are up in the ranks."

"There is a huge difference between a positive and a negative response, Kels."

"On the flip side, who is going to tell me the truth being that it's such a huge secret? Normally I wouldn't care. I have to have thick skin being in the public eye, but something is pulling me to figure it all out." Kelsey shifted in her seat. "Maybe we could make a good use of the trip to the castle tomorrow seeing as the scandal all began there. Just think; we could make it into the history books!" She laughed.

"Oh no, don't you drag me into this wild idea. I don't look good in stripes." Beth shuddered.

"How would I get along without you? You can solve any design problem in the world!" She attempted to stroke her ego.

Beth adjusted her glasses. "It's not… illegal is it?"

She switched to high gear with a smug grin and sped off.

They pulled up to Beth's modest ranch home in the suburbs. Kelsey's phone buzzed. She flipped the top open and scrolled down to read the text message. "Oh, fun!"

"What's going on?" Beth leaned over to read it.

"Her Majesty's Personal Assistant wants me to meet her at the palace air strip. She wants me to take a helicopter to the Lord's grounds and guess who gets to come with me?"

"You know I have a fear of heights! I'd rather take the stinky, crowded bus. Are you sure we can't go the normal way?" Beth whined.

"Sorry, you're best friends with royalty and there are some things you must do."

"I didn't sign up for this when we became friends."

"And I didn't sign up to be a part of this family." She turned to Beth. "I'm not sure what I did without you before you moved here!"

Chapter 2

Beth looked in her small stuffed closet for clothes that could endure the whipping winds of the helicopter blades. "I can't believe I'm doing this!" She checked her watch and groaned.

She quickly picked out a pair of black pants and a button down shirt with a sweater vest. She grabbed a hair tie and wound her unruly hair into a tight bun.

"You made it! I was beginning to wonder if you were going to chicken out!" Kelsey handed her a helmet.

The pilot flipped some switches and the blades began to rotate.

"I feel so much better knowing my hat matches my pants!" Beth's sarcasm was barely audible.

The girls jumped up into the plush seats and buckled. Kelsey motioned to use the tiny microphone attached to the helmet to speak to one another. "It will only take us fifteen minutes to get there."

The servant shut the doors to the choper and ran back toward the tower. The noise drowned out any other. Beth watched as the ground became further away and the tree tops glistened in the sun light.

Kelsey smiled and felt the freedom of flight. She looked out the window and saw a farmer plowing the rich, dark soil. The cars appeared like shiny bugs following the leader. Kelsey wasn't sure how the day would play out, but held high hopes of finding something, anything that linked her to her family's past.

Beth sensed her wonderment. "Do you feel alright?"

"I just want to know where I came from and put a stop to the rumors. After centuries, it is about time the speculations ended. It is so frustrating hearing whispers in corners and knowing only as much as the public does."

"What is that?" Beth glanced downward.

"It looks like an old graveyard and tiny church. I can see the cross on the roof."

"If walls could talk." Beth pondered.

The helicopter then circled around a tall, stone castle.

"It is only a fourth the size of the palace, but doesn't it look magnificent?" Kelsey's face beamed with excitement. "Those are the west gardens and over there are the east ones. I've seen pictures of them in the Palace's drawing room," she pointed out to Beth.

They could see gigantic, hundred year old trees surrounded by rose bushes and fountains. A mossy path connected the two very private sanctuaries.

They could make out the crowd of fellow classmates gathering next to the big, yellow bus parked half a mile north of the castle.

"Looks like we made it on time." Kelsey replied.

"That ride wasn't as bad as I thought." Beth unbuckled after the aircraft had landed.

Kelsey was hoping the same thing about uncovering the mysteries that might torment her forever.

They joined the line forming at the gate of the castle. Kelsey could see the slate driveway with lush, green moss growing in between the cracks. She wiggled and goose bumps formed on her slender arms.

"It's going to be okay." Beth tried to convince not only Kelsey, but herself.

"I guess. I have an odd feeling about this place."

"Ladies, stay together during this tour. No one is allowed to step away and venture far from the group. Our tour guide will be Mrs. Short from the Historical Society. It should take a few hours. At the request of Her Majesty, the chef will prepare an exquisite dinner for us in the formal dining room before we get back on the bus." Their teacher strained her soft spoken voice as loud as she could to the twenty girls in line.

An elderly man approached in worn overalls and a shovel. He threw the tool to the side and unlocked the tall, wrought iron gate. His hands dirty from gardening, wrapped around its bars, prying them apart. It squeaked with resistance and the girls covered their ears from the shrill, painful noise.

Their teacher waved her hands for her class to enter toward the seventeenth century mansion.

Kelsey and Beth skipped past the gardener and his mouth dropped open. He quickly closed the entrance and hobbled at a fast pace toward the side of the castle.

Kelsey pursed her lips together attempting to understand his reaction. *I keep forgetting.* She spoke to herself. *My dad does hold the Viscount title. Although I am in a low peerage, to him that must be like seeing a celebrity. Being that he works here and I gather it has been for quite some time, I'm sure he has seen me in a family portrait.*

Mrs. Short met them at the front door and had them cluster around her in the circular foyer. It stretched three stories upward and was decorated in gold and silver. The colors were on separate stones beneath their feet and began to swirl in a unique pattern up the walls.

The middle of the dome held the family crest with the two hues so intricately interlaid, that one could only make out the thin, separate strands from the sun light streaming through the tiny, vertical windows in the third story of the structure.

Mrs. Short glanced at each girl and opened her mouth to speak. She hesitated when her eyes met Kelsey's, and fumbled on her words attempting to remember her speech from past tours.

Kelsey peered over at Beth who was busy looking around the room. *Goodness, I know I'm part of the Royal Family, but I have no title, no one else pays attention to me let alone the main family line. Why am I so shocking to them? I almost feel like I have the plague or something.* She nudged Beth with her elbow.

"Ouch!" Beth shot her a gaze through smoldering, thin slits.

Mrs. Short cast her brows upward at Beth. "I ask you remain respectful and quiet during our visit. You may ask questions by raising your hands."

Kelsey's head hung low. "Sorry, you seemed so caught up in all this. I'm feeling really uncomfortable right now. Everyone is looking at me like I'm some sort of alien. You would have thought I had no right to be here."

"Oh, don't get your panties in a bunch!" Beth whispered back. "They are just shocked because this is one of your family's estates. No mystery there." She rolled her eyes.

"Yeah, maybe you're right. But just in case, I might as well ask the next person who reacts strangely to me."

"You have an insatiable curiosity. You know, that killed the cat."

"Stop being so dramatic." Kelsey quipped. "Besides, what is the harm in asking questions? Mrs. Short said we could."

Beth wondered if Kelsey was trying to find something that wasn't there. As a friend, she accepted that was just one of Kelsey's flaws. God knew she had several of her own. "Fine, then let's go have fun with our imaginations." Beth gave in.

Kelsey smiled back knowing she understood her better than anyone else. She heard a muffled buzz coming from her hand clutch. She quickly distanced herself from the group to answer her cell phone.

"Kelsey?" A young, woman's voice questioned.

"Yes."

"This is Abie Hall, Her Majesty's Personal Assistant."

Kelsey had seen her name written in several news clippings but had never met or seen her. She heard a light sound of harp strings being plucked in the caller's background.

"I have a very important proposition for you as directed from the Queen. She has had several people attempt to find the Princess Royale a suitable, potential husband. We were wondering if you might be able to under take this seeing as she is not able to go places in the public sector where you, who hold no title, can."

"I can try my best. I'm sure you know that I attend an all-girl's school."

"Yes, but you will be out for summer soon and have all the time in the world to give attention to this matter."

"Alright, I'll try, but I'm not promising anything," Kelsey ended the conversation.

Beth had followed her away from the group and had overheard the discussion. "How are you going to do *that*?" Her freckles scrunched up on her diminutive nose.

Kelsey's eyes widened. "I have no idea, but I have to admit, it feels good to be needed by my family. I just wish I could be accepted and wanted for being me."

Mrs. Short escorted the group into the gigantic, medieval-meets-modern kitchen. Several metal counters lined the middle of the room with overly sized appliances. Kelsey counted four stoves and fridges.

"Although no one lives here anymore, the Royal Family has a staff of ten who attend to meeting all the needs of the guests who visit. They are creating a scrumptious feast for us." Mrs. Short pointed to the cooks shuffling and bustling in a hurried sweat. Pots boiled, chopping noises echoed and spoons clanked against pans. A combination of smells permeated the moist air.

"Lynn?" Mrs. Short attempted to get the attention of one of the chefs.

The round woman covered in all white looked up from the sink and quickly came over.

"Yes, mum?" Little pieces of white hair poked out from her hat.

"I would like to introduce you all to Lynn McCreedy. She is the Head Chef. This title has been in her family for decades. She has continued the recipes which have been past down to her since the times of Duke Rupert Dane."

Mrs. McCreedy's plump cheeks blushed into a deep rose.

"Thank you, mum." She bowed.

"Onward toward the bed chambers." Mrs. Short led the line of girls.

Mrs. McCreedy's smile turned once she saw Kelsey. Her eyes held concern and she frowned, revealing the wrinkles around her thin lips.

"That is it!" Kelsey's frustration could not be squelched any longer.

Beth shook her head and watched her friend confront the Head Chef.

"Mrs. McCreedy?" Kelsey asked.

"Y-y-yes?" She stammered through crooked teeth.

"Do you know my name?"

The woman nodded slowly.

"Why do you look at me this way? I should be asking, why has everyone who works here look at me with such surprise? Don't I have the right to be here?" Her aggression grew.

The Chef took a step back. "Come with me." She said looking around to make sure no one was watching them slip away. She scurried them into a large pantry, lit a few candles and closed the door.

At that moment, Beth found herself wondering if there really was something to Kelsey's intrigue.

"I'm weak. I admit it. They only keep me 'round because I'm the only one who knows the family recipes. I'm nicely tucked away here in the kitchen." She wiped the trickle of perspiration from her forehead. "No one has ever gotten the spunk to ask me anything but what my career entails."

"You have to tell me what is going on. I have no title or pull." She tried to reason with the woman to convince her to disclose what she was hiding.

"I'm sure it's just a myth. Ye know; I heard it from my mum who heard it from her mum and the likes." She hesitated to continue, but knew nothing could be proven. The evidence was covered up and no one would hear what she was about to say. She couldn't keep the secret any longer.

"Have you heard the rumors?" She didn't want to tell Kelsey anymore than she had to if she hadn't heard of them in the first place.

"Yes. In fact," She turned to Beth, "We heard whisperings of it just yesterday. How can you and others go around saying things that may very well be untrue? It's revolting. What if I did that to your family?"

"You don't have to. My family line is already tarnished." She lowered her eyes.

Mrs. McCreedy motioned for the girls to come closer and began to speak softly. "Duke Dane was the nephew of the King at the time. The King had one daughter who refused to marry and wanted to renounce her possessions and become a nun against her father's demands to remain at the main castle. She continued her pious works. His sons weren't able to take the throne. The King was ill and so approached Duke Dane to continue the bloodline."

Her Celtic accent thickened. "The Duke had a secret romance at the time with Azuriah-a commoner. It was scandalous. My great, great grand mum found them stealing kisses in the west garden behind the tall shrubs. They thought they were alone." She paused with a sigh.

"Go on." Kelsey gently urged her.

"To convince the King that the Duke would make a good replacement, his friend, Trestan Stowe, who later turned out to be his enemy, thought he should be seen by a doctor to determine if he could continue the bloodline. The results came back as infertile."

Kelsey and Beth shook their heads.

"Some wonder if Trestan tampered with the results." Mrs. McCreedy scratched her brow. "The King would not allow the Duke to marry Azuriah so the Duke vowed *never* to marry."

"Although, a funny thing happened." She tapped her index finger against her chin. "A month later, the Duke wed a woman no one had ever seen or heard of. Not even a painting was made of her. Roughly nine months later they had a baby boy they named Graham. A post was sent out that the Duchess passed away giving birth. He never remarried."

"Wait, so am I hearing that you wonder if the Duchess ever existed?"

Mrs. McCreedy dodged the question. "I'm sure it's all a myth. Like that would really happen? Sounds like something out of a soap opera."

"No. It sounds like life. We are not in Heaven. Things definitely go askew and they don't always turn out the way you want them to." Beth interjected.

"If this woman never existed, then where did Graham come from?" Kelsey prodded.

"I'm not gonna tell ye anythin'. Ye won't believe it unless ye learn it for yeself."

"The truth needs to be told." Kelsey pleaded

"Yes, but no one can prove it, so it will always be a myth."

"Mrs. McCreedy?" The Sous-Chef yelled.

"I've got to go. I do feel better having told someone." She cracked the door, being able to see the kitchen with one eye.

"I will walk out first with a bag of flour." She said taking the container off a shelf. "Give me a few minutes. I will create a diversion and the two of ye swiftly sneak out and join the rest of your group."

The girls ran behind the door as she opened it most of the way to return to the kitchen. She closed the door behind her.

"We've got to find out what happened." Kelsey pointed out.

"As she was telling the story I thought something was amidst too, but it turns out he did marry and was able to continue the lineage. It sounds to me that the test results were wrong."

"Maybe and maybe not. Hang in there with me on this one." Kelsey sighed. "I feel like this is only the begining."

"Mrs. McCreedy already said there was nothing to be found. How can you prove something without any evidence?"

"She said the Duke and Azuriah used to go to the west gardens together. It's a start."

Suddenly they heard a loud commotion coming from the kitchen. All became quiet and then someone began hitting a spoon several times against a metal triangle.

"Is that our signal to leave?" Beth inquired.

"Out! Out, everyone except Mrs. McCreedy!" A woman's voice rang harsh.

Kelsey placed her arm in front of Beth. "I don't think this part was planned."

They stood in the darkness and listened to an argument of emotion erupt between the two quieted voices. Every now and then the girls could make out a word.

"You are to leave at once!" A woman's voice declared.

Another sentence of jabber was barely audible, and then they heard crying.

Beth peeked into the bright light of the kitchen to see Mrs. McCreedy now alone and sobbing. They ran out of the pantry and over to her.

"What happened?"

She wouldn't speak, but motioned for the girls to leave and continued to cry.

Beth and Kelsey quickly tip toed out of the kitchen and through several rooms before they stopped to catch their breath in what looked to be a sitting room.

Floral tapestries adorned the loveseats surrounding a number of small mahogany tables. A window seat overlooked the east gardens. The wood floor creaked under their small feet. They both collapsed on a burgundy velvet chaise on the far side of the room.

"My heart is pounding." Beth attempted to slow her breathing.

"Mine too. Why do you suppose Mrs. McCreedy was let go?"

"Who was speaking to her?"

"You don't think someone is on to our trail do you?" Kelsey's anxiety heightened.

"What trail?"

"Well, Mrs. McCreedy did reveal quite a bit to us," Kelsey reminded her.

"No one saw us go into the pantry with her did they?" Beth asked.

Kelsey wiped the sweat from her forehead. "Not unless one of the cooks did and told someone."

"I think we're getting too carried away. That couldn't have been the reason," Beth postulated. "Our imaginations are going a little wild. That is all."

"Her Majesty did know I'd be here today. Do you think she sent someone to keep tabs on me so I wouldn't find out the truth?" Kelsey asked.

They heard the click clack of high heels far down the hall.

"Listen. They're getting closer," Kelsey warned.

"Just in case, let's hide." Beth grabbed Kelsey's arm and they covered themselves behind the yards of fabric hanging from each side of the window seat that created billows on the floor, concealing their feet from view.

They heard the woman with the heels enter the tea room and pause. Kelsey could barely make out the figure. The lady walked closer to the windows and then meandered back toward the door, shutting it as she left.

They waited in silence until the sound of her heels drifted away. They both popped out from behind the curtains.

"Do you think she locked us in?" Beth asked.

"I hope not." Kelsey ran to turn the knob. It rotated all the way around. She let out a huge sigh.

"That was close," Beth's voice quivered. "I think we should stop looking into this and go find the group."

"Are you kidding me?" Kelsey's interest peaked.

"We almost got locked in a room without food and water and when someone finally would have found us, we'd be in a heap of trouble!"

Kelsey halted. "I'm not going to let fear keep me from finding out the truth that may bring my family closer together."

"Do you really think it will bring you all closer when someone is trying to stop you from finding out?"

"The lies need to be dissolved. Secrets create separation in families. I want there to be unity. The truth will bring us all back together." Kelsey placed her hands on Beth's shoulders. "I'll make a deal with you. If we don't find a shred of evidence, I'll stop this silly charade." She held out her hand.

"Deal." Beth took her hand and shook it.

Kelsey arched her brow. "Now let's go find the West Gardens."

Chapter 3

They found a stairwell that led to a door at the back of the castle. The fresh air plunged inward at them blowing the sides of Kelsey's hair. They found themselves on a large cement patio overlooking the pond.

Beth nervously looked back at the house hoping no one saw them come out. A shadowy figure caught her attention in a third story window then vanished. She shook it off and hoped she was seeing things. Since she couldn't be sure, she decided not to rile Kelsey.

"Do you know which way is west?" Kelsey asked.

"Lucky for you I used to be a girl scout in America. The sun will tell you." She pointed up in the cloudless sky. "To our right."

They strolled through several arbors with pink and red roses overtaking the wooden beams, blocking the brightness from their eyes. The sweet smell lingered in their noses.

"This is heaven. Could you imagine actually living here?" Kelsey dreamed for an instant.

They came across a smaller pond with a bridge arching across it. They skipped over it and came to a solid mass of ten foot high hedging.

"Right or left?" Beth asked.

Kelsey looked both ways and propped her back against the thick twigs. She glanced toward the house to see their school group entering out onto the patio. "We've gotta hide and fast!"

"Do you think we could go through the brush?" Beth wondered.

"Not without scrapes," Kelsey added.

"I wouldn't mind those compared to getting caught!"

Kelsey and Beth searched the thick foliage to find a place that had the best opening and squeezed their way into the mass cluster of greenery. Twigs pulled at their clothes and snagged on their hair.

"Break some of the branches in front of you as you go." Beth hoped she wouldn't get an eye poked out.

"I'm trying." Kelsey struggled and pushed herself through to the other side falling onto the grass with fresh bruises. She looked up and saw three fountains shooting several feet into the air all illuminated with rainbows from the sunlight. A few old willow trees towered over the corners of the garden.

"You didn't want to use the gate to get in?" A low voice laughed next to her.

She screamed, startled by this unexpected man.

He knelt down and extended his large hand. "I'm Brody Bronson." His wide, pearly smile stretched from one side of his face to the other show casing his dimple in the middle of his chin.

"Kelsey Dane." She blew her hair out of her face. Twigs and leaves had created snarls in her locks.

"I have the pleasure of meeting a royal?"

"N-No. I'm a far off version on the family tree."

"Kelsey, I'm stuck could you help pull me out?" Beth shouted.

Brody quickly helped Kelsey to her feet and she brushed herself off.

"Gotta go help a friend." She pointed, noticing his short, wavy hair blowing in the breeze like fields of golden wheat. She suddenly felt weak in the knees unable to hide her attraction to him.

She ran over to where Beth was, almost tripping in her preoccupation of this guy. Kelsey figured he must be one of the garden tenders.

She ripped a few pieces of shrubbery to get Beth loose and pulled her leg with all her might. The momentum hurled Beth onto a perfectly cut, grass walk way around the edge of the garden. Kelsey landed on her back. Brody ran over to the both of them.

"I know what you are thinking," Kelsey spoke to the guy. "You are going to have to repair that and how dare we make you work harder than you already have to. Sorry." She smiled coquettishly.

He belted out a roar of laughter holding his stomach. "You think...I…work here?" He paused between chuckles.

Oh, man, what have I gotten myself into? Kelsey nibbled on her thumb nail. "Well, who are you?"

"I'm the Earl of Atherton. I'm studying exotic plants for my botany degree. These gardens are amazing." He waved his hands in the air at the expansiveness.

Suddenly it hit her like a pile of bricks. The Queen's assistant had requested she find her cousin Princess Victoria a match. This guy held the right title and how could she resist his looks? *He's educated and…stop, stop, stop. Not for you, Kelsey.* She spoke to herself. "Hey, you're not married or engaged are you?"

"Wow! I've had lots of women come on to me but none that blunt." He was taken aback.

"Not for me silly, for my cousin, the Princess Royale. Heard of her?"

"Oh." He peered down.

"Great. I'm sensing my work is cut out for me. Just one date with her? She is a real sweetheart or so I've been told. Think of how you could benefit the botany world in that peerage position?" Kelsey pointed a finger at him.

"I wish I could have someone find me a handsome, rich and kind husband." Beth declared.

Kelsey shot her a glare. "You're not helping."

"How am I supposed to help? I don't know the Princess, but what I do know is how cute the two of you look together."

"I think so too." Brody put his arm around Kelsey's shoulders.

She pushed him away jokingly. "Seriously though, will you try it, for me?"

"I guess I can do that for you." He sighed with frustration then changed the subject. "I want to show you girls what I'm working on right now."

They followed him through the ferns and lilacs. Layers of different flowers circled a cement gazebo tucked behind topiaries.

"It's so private on this side." Kelsey admitted.

"Look." He led them up the stairs and into the gazebo where they could see the whole garden. The long arms of the willows hid them from view.

"It's like a tree house, except a lot more stable." Beth tried to shake the steady railing.

"Now, to show you what I've been studying." He took them back down the stairs and pointed to the rows of unusual flowers. They all knelt down. He gently cupped a purple petal in his hand. "I planted this hybrid here to see if it could handle the PH of the soil and only partial sun.

Kelsey cocked her head as the rays hit something shiny in the soil. She started digging at it with her hand to uncover the rest of it.

"What are you doing?" Brody put his hand on her arm. "Don't dig them up."

Tingles raced up and down her forearm. She hesitated and shook the feeling coming over her. "I found something in the dirt." She replied.

"You mean soil," he corrected her.

"Whatever." They watched as she raised a blue, cloisonné, tear drop earring.

"That looks old. I wonder how long it's been there." Beth contemplated. Then she started tapping Kelsey on the back and they looked at each other with the same thought as they often had.

Kelsey nodded and opened her clutch, withdrawing a Kleenex. She wiped the dirt off of it, and placed it safely in one of the purse's pockets.

"Finder's keepers." Brody said. "What do you want with one, old earring?"

Beth looked up at the waning sun and remembered that the group would soon be gathering for dinner. "We have to rejoin our class. They'll know we're gone if we don't show up at the table."

"Give me a number where I can reach you and I'll set something up with Princess Victoria." She handed Brody a pen and paper.

He quickly jotted it down and gave it to her. "Nice meeting you two. Oh, and the garden gate is over there." He directed them keeping his eyes on Kelsey.

Once they were out of ear shot Beth spoke up. "Now what?"

"Let me think." Kelsey said.

"We don't have much time. The castle doors close at dusk. How do you know if the earring belonged to Azuriah or not?" Beth asked.

Kelsey started to bite her nails.

Beth took her friend's hand down from her mouth.

"Nervous habit." Kelsey shrugged.

"This kind of seems like a dead end." Beth admitted.

"The truth could bring justice to the love that the Duke and Azuriah shared," Kelsey's sentiments surfaced. "Plus, it would be insane to stop here. You know it would nag us forever if we let this go."

"I can't stand it when you're right."

"There must be a record of their love somewhere. What about letters? Where would he have kept them?" Kelsey began nibbling on her lower lip.

"Is there a study or office in the castle?" Beth asked.

"I like the way your mind works. This is the first time I've been here so we'll have to search."

They began running toward the mansion. The heels of Kelsey's shoes kept sinking in the dirt, slowing her down. She flung them off and dangled the backs from her fingers.

Beth modeled her behavior. "This will help us be much quieter while sneaking around the rooms."

"That sounds so sinister."Kelsey replied.

"It's open to the public for goodness sake! It's meant to be looked at."

They made their way into a side entrance and into the cool shade of the first floor. A gentle stringed instrument could be heard from a room nearby.

"What's that?" Beth asked.

"A harp." Kelsey recalled as they ambled closer. Then it dawned on her. In the background of Abie Hall's phone call a harp could be heard.

Did she call her from inside the castle? Is she the one spying on us? I wonder if the Queen instructed her to watch our every move. This will be harder than I thought. "We need to find the study fast!" Kelsey whispered and looked back at Beth still lingering down the hall.

"I think I found it!"

Kelsey silently walked toward Beth. She had already opened the door half way.

"Get in here." Beth swatted at the air. "Go to the desk."

Kelsey began feverishly opening all the drawers while Beth stood guard. "They're locked!"

Beth took a bobby pin from her hair and threw it at Kelsey's open hands. "Use this."

"I've never picked anything in my life."

"Put it in the key hole and wiggle it until it pops open." Beth instructed.

"Where did you learn that? Never mind. I probably don't want to know." She jiggled one loose and opened it. "It's empty." She said with disappointment. She tried all the others with the same result. "This isn't working." Kelsey paused in deep thought.

Kelsey plopped on the floor and looked underneath. It was dark and hard to see. She glided her fingers along the bottom edges of the drawers. She felt a loose, thin paper stuffed into the seam of the large desk and tugged at it gently. It came out with little effort. She stood up and looked at it near the arched window. "I think I got it."

Beth left her post and hurried over to examine the find. The words were faded and hard to make out. The cursive handwriting had a feminine quality.

The door to the study flew all the way open and a petite, twenty- something lady stood in the doorway. Beth quickly slipped the letter into her pocket.

The woman's sandy blonde, shoulder length hair was neatly combed under. Her slender face held tiny, beady eyes.

"Kelsey, I'm Abie Hall. At last we meet." She came closer to shake hands. She looked all around them and at the objects in the room. "This was Duke Dane's study; nothing of interest in here. Let me show you something that will intrigue you."

She placed her hands on the girl's backs leading them out of the study. Abie turned around to lock the door and grinned knowingly.

Abie took the girls into the long dining room with their classmates already sitting at the table awaiting the first course. "You are just in time for dinner. Afterwards we'll gather in the exhibit room to go over the historical artifacts the Duke left as our legacy."

She watched Beth and Kelsey as they settled into the intricately carved, dark wood chairs before leaving to report back to the Queen.

"You'll be happy to know I intervened." Abie informed. "They were snooping around, but I am certain they have found nothing. Besides, five years ago I managed the team that scoured the place and all the artifacts are now safely enclosed in the exhibit room. I will keep an eye on these medaling girls, Your Majesty. Your secrets are safe with me."

"We need a place to view these documents." Kelsey spoke under her breath between bites. They had just brought out the cream of mushroom soup and cranberry apple salads.

"Mrs. Short will most likely give us all a bathroom break after dinner. We'll sneak out then." Beth replied.

"Where? Abie knows this place better than we do. She could have her watchful eye on us from several locations."

"Not necessarily. We'll stay in the bathroom until everyone else has gone. Oh, I've got a better idea." Beth paused. "Abie won't go in the men's bathroom. This whole tour is full of girls. No one will be in there!"

"My goodness, you're a genius!"

After the luxurious meal of orange duck in saffron sauce and stuffing, they requested a bathroom break. After all had left to head down to the exhibit room, they raced into the men's privy and hid in a stall to read the letters.

Beth put the lid down. They stood on top of it and knelt so no one could see their feet. She pulled out the crinkled paper and straightened it.

Kelsey could not believe her eyes. She had been right that they had exchanged love letters. "Look, this one was while they were courting." She began to quietly read aloud. "

"Dearest Rupert,

How can I express what you mean to me? Of course I will be forever yours. I could never love another.

I replay in my mind the night we ran away from the crowd into the garden. You were and always will be my first and last kiss. The moonlight shined upon us and I felt God blessing our love.

I thought I saw someone see us unless it was my imagination. Next time we have to be more discreet. I seemed to have lost my cloisonné earring. Do you have it as a keepsake perhaps? Meet me in the meadow by the lake after church.

Love for all time,

Azuriah"

"The other was decades later." Beth pointed to the date written on the letters. "All of them from his true love, Azuriah."

Kelsey read the next one.

"Dearest Duke Rupert Dane,

I write to you with sadness. I heard of your wedding to the Duchess and have to remind myself that your love for me is gone. Every day thoughts of you cross my mind. The Lord brought us together and the devil tore us apart. I will never understand. I have a daughter now. Her name is Flora. She is so jovial and gay, just like we used to be.

With all my love,

Azuriah"

"She married and had a child with another? Why did she do that when she was so deeply in love with the Duke?" Kelsey shuddered.

"It must have been the same reason *he* married someone else." Beth replied.

Kelsey could not understand. "Then who did he marry and where are *his* wife's love letters?"

"Maybe it was arranged and they didn't have those types of feelings for each other."

"Why would he throw his love away?" Kelsey asked.

"She was a commoner and it was his duty to be King." Beth postulated.

"Do you remember that graveyard we saw from the helicopter right before we landed?" Kelsey asked.

"Yeah."

"If we go there, we might be able to figure out who they each married. Flora might be there too and we could compare last names." Kelsey's mind was a blur of ideas.

"Those would be pretty old and hard to read," Beth said.

"You can do rubbings. All you have to do is put some paper over them and rub the chalk until it reveals the letters and numbers."

"It's starting to get dark out. I can't imagine you have a flash light?" Beth asked.

"Who needs one? It's supposed to be a full moon tonight."

Chapter 4

"It's starting to get chilly out here. Are you sure you know where we're going?" Kelsey began to doubt Beth's directions.

"Yes. I remember it was at an oblique angle from the west gardens. It should only be another half mile."

They sloshed through the tall, wet grass.

"We are going to get in so much trouble. Mrs. Short, Abie Hall and our teacher will see that we are missing." Kelsey pushed the reeds out of her way.

"They don't know where to find us plus you can summon the helicopter to take us home when we've found what we're looking for," Beth determined.

Kelsey sat down on a large rock. "I'm beginning to wonder what that is anymore."

"How many times have you told me, Kels? It's the truth. Bring your family back together. That is why I'm helping you on this wild journey."

Kelsey hugged her friend. "Thanks for being there for me and reminding me what is important in life."

"Can I remind you of something else?" Beth asked.

"What?"

"Brody likes you back."

"Uhh." She socked Beth in the arm. "You know he'd be better off with the Princess Royale. She had to earn the Royale part. She has everything a guy would want. Besides, once he meets her, he'll forget about me. He'll get caught up in it."

"Do you really think he's that type of guy?" Beth's gut told her he wasn't.

"Perhaps," Kelsey replied

Beth clenched her fists in anger. "Do you think that low of yourself that he wouldn't want you?"

"Yes, I have self esteem issues, but I'm looking at it objectively." Kelsey's insecurity got the best of her.

"What you have to offer him is true love – just like Duke Dane and Azuriah. You could learn a thing or two from them," Beth attempted to reason with her.

"I already told him I would set him up. If it doesn't go well, then I'll consider it, but only if he brings it up. What about you? You seem to push guys away," Kelsey turned the conversation.

"Well, if Miss Matchmaker would set *me* up with someone, I would have the opportunity to rectify that." Beth secretly missed her ex-boyfriend, Demitri. "I see the steeple of the church. The graveyard is just on the other side of it."

"Thank God. My legs feel like they are about to fall off with all that running around we've been doing." Kelsey pushed on.

They approached the small chapel.

"It looks like there are only about twenty or so gravestones," Beth estimated. "This shouldn't be too hard to find."

"Are you sure we should even touch them? It looks like they're ready to crumble," Kelsey observed.

"Just do your best." Beth handed her some chalk and paper they got from the Mrs. Short's desk at the castle.

The fog began to settle toward the earth and the paper felt clammy. "Beth, come here." She excitedly proclaimed. "F-L-O." She rubbed some more. "Come on." She prayed. "R –A."

Beth had already dropped what she was doing to examine Kelsey's find. "What is the last name?"

"Does it matter? It would have changed if she got married."

"Sometimes, especially if the stone was purchased before her marriage, they might have the maiden name on it. For instance, if she had a disease, yet recovered? Do you get my meaning there?"

"Yes and that is terrible."

"It is just how things were done in this country back then," Beth recalled from a past history class.

Kelsey hesitated before revealing the last name. It slowly came to view. "Telton."

"Now we have to find Azuriah's and see if it matches." Beth was able to find it and the last names were the same.

"I want to do a rubbing of that big one in the middle." Kelsey stared in awe. "Whose do you suppose it is?"

"Nobility probably; all of the people with royal titles were buried in a separate cemetery." Beth concluded.

Kelsey began to reveal the letters on it. "R-U-P-E-R-T D-A-." As she finished she realized it was her relative. "This is him. Why would he chose to be buried here and not with the other royals? Was he not King when he passed?" She asked rhetorically.

"This was his family home and church though." Beth said while working on another grave. "I found Graham."

Kelsey quickly raced to the site. "His birth date is the same as Flora's. Do you think that means anything?"

"Don't churches have records?"

"Yes, they do!" Kelsey ran over to the doors and tried to open them. They were locked.

Beth felt the tops of the door frame for a skeleton key. Nothing.

Kelsey looked under a few rocks only to find roly poly bugs. Then she saw a crack and felt cold metal. She pulled a skeleton key out and tried the lock. It opened. No one was around and all the candles were blown out.

"If we leave the entry wide open, the moon light will shine in." Beth placed a large rock against the door so it wouldn't close.

"Where would they keep the records?" Kelsey asked seeing only pews and the pulpit.

"Is there a trap door or shelter?" Beth asked

"I don't know," Kelsey replied. "You look on that side and I'll scan this area."

They met up in the center and felt unevenness under the runner down the middle of the church. Kelsey pulled back the fabric and unveiled a wooden planked door with a silver, circle handle. "I'm scared! What if there are spiders?"

"It's too dark. I'll look for something to light the candles." Beth searched in the sand filled box attached to the candle holders. She found long match sticks and lit ten of them. "I'll go down."

"And leave me alone up here? I guess I'll have to get over my fear," Kelsey determined.

They cautiously descended the four wooden steps that led to a dirt bottom basement.

"I wonder when this church was built." Beth loved history as much as her uncle.

There were wooden shelves a few feet off the ground, reaching to the short ceiling.

They dug through old parchment papers searching for the names.

"Oh my, this is so sad." Kelsey held up the paper to the light. "Here is a document that requests Azuriah be buried in this cemetery according to King Rupert Dane's wish."

"Huh, looks like they got to be together after all." Beth mused.

"That was *so* not funny."

"What I meant was that now they are in heaven, they will be together forever." Beth reclaimed her thoughts.

Suddenly, they heard a loud boom.

"Was that thunder?" Kelsey hoped.

Heavy footsteps shook the floor above them.

They clung to each other praying for strength. They peered toward the hatch with eyes only half way open. Then an older man's head adorned with sprigs of gray hair appeared gazing in through the basement's hatch.

"H-h-hello?" Kelsey tried being cordial though fear had shaken her to the core.

"I saw the candle light flickering in the windows from afar." His baritone voice vibrated. "Then when I came to check it out, I found the doors held open with rocks. You could imagine my surprise." He miffed. "I'm the caretaker here and you are trespassing."

"We're so sorry. I figured it was okay since these are public records. The church just happened to be locked. We couldn't come at normal business hours." Kelsey tried to appeal to his forgiving side.

"*They* know you're here and want you to stop your searching or bad things will befall you both! Now get out!" He screamed.

The girls waited until he left them space to climb back out of the basement, and they ran like the wind toward the castle, never looking back.

They caught their breath on a large rock a few hundred yards from the estate.

"Maybe we should stop." Kelsey suggested.

"Now look who is the adventurous one. You started this mess." Beth chirped.

"What? This has nothing to do with you and you could've said no at anytime."

Beth shook her head. "I'm sorry."

"Me too, I just can't help but wonder if it's worth the fight as things get more intense."

"Family is always worth the fight. So are friends and boyfriends as long as their feelings are reciprocated." Beth said.

Kelsey gathered strength from her holy spirit. “If we are not going to stop this charade, I’d better buck up and think of the next step.”

“I’m all out of ideas. You need to lead. I’m just willing to go along for the ride and when I’m old I’ll be able to say that I was there.” Beth smiled.

“Ha, ha, I’m intrigued to see if the castle has a library.” Kelsey said.

Beth cocked her head. “In the mood to read some poetry?”

“More like records of family history or even a family tree.”

“Now I get it. You know, after all this is done, maybe we should open up a detective agency.” Beth smiled with a fanatical gleam.

“I think I’ll stick with the culinary arts and without you as a designer, where on Earth would people be able to find amazing clothes?” Kelsey commented.

“Oh, so true.”

Chapter 5

Kelsey checked her watch. "It is nine o'clock at night. My parents aren't expecting me back home till late because of this field trip."

"My mom and dad will get worried soon if I don't arrive before ten." Beth's voice grew tense.

"I'll phone for the choper to pick us up in forty five minutes. That should give us enough time to search the library." Kelsey reached into her purse and dialed the pilot. "All set." She ended the call.

"Wait. I thought the estate closed at dusk?" Beth recalled.

"It only closes for tour groups. The staff doesn't go home until everything is cleaned and put back together." Kelsey said.

"I saw a map of the building by the front desk," Beth added.

"Great start."

They made their way through the darkened halls and arrived at the dimly lit office.

"There it is on the wall like I saw before. According to the map, the library is on the second floor. We could take the elevator or the stairs." Beth postulated.

"Considering I'm pretty exhausted, I vouch for the elevator."

They went to the room adjacent to the office and pushed the 'up' button. "Since when do medieval castles have elevators?"

"At this point I don't really care, but it might say inside." Kelsey said.

The doors opened with a resounding ding. They walked into the very modern and spacious lift.

"Here you go. The sign says they added this feature four years ago." Beth read.

"Now I can go home happy."

The doors closed. They began to rise a few seconds and then stopped.

"What's going on?" Beth pushed the second floor button again. Still nothing.

Kelsey inhaled a deep breath. "Let's just be patient." Minutes went by.

"Now I'm going to freak out." Beth was nervous of small spaces and this was not the best situation. She pushed the open doors button and tried prying them apart.

"Glad you think you're super woman, but I doubt that even a bodybuilder could do that," Kelsey deducted

Beth glared. "What do you suppose we do sleuth?"

Kelsey calmly pointed up at the trap door on the roof of the elevator. "Since you are flipping out right now, I'll hoist you up first. Once you get on top of it, reach your arm down and help pull me up."

"Thank God there is a way out!" Beth exclaimed.

They did just as Kelsey had instructed. Once they were both in the cavity of the lift, they used the cable to shimmy up to the roof where there was a door directly above them. "We'll have to use the stairs to climb back to the second floor."

"I'm just happy we're outta there!" Beth panted. "Do you think someone tried to stop us or was it a malfunction?"

"Your guess is as good as mine."

The girls found the library and flipped a power switch. Mahogany book cases lined every inch of the walls. They began digging through them. Beth found an envelope between two dusty books and opened it.

"What 'cha got?" Kelsey inquired.

Beth read it aloud in an audible whisper.

"Dear Duke Dane,

You are requested to meet with me privately at Castle Rutherford. The staff will be awaiting your arrival. This is of grave importance and you must come immediately.

You're Highness"

Kelsey sighed. "It even has the crown seal."

"Here is the game plan. After we wake tomorrow morning, we need to drive out to Castle Rutherford," Beth said.

"How will we gain access to his private meeting room? We don't even know where it is." Kelsey leaned against the back of a reading chair.

"Think on it tonight. I'll meet you at ten a.m.," Beth instructed.

"Good." Kelsey hesitated. "That will give me enough time to contact Abie with Brody's information."

"Are you serious? You're going to feed him to the wolf?" Beth couldn't believe what she was hearing.

"You can't prove that Abie stopped the elevator." Kelsey struggled to believe. "No, but she certainly proved she doesn't want us snooping around and I'm starting to wonder why," Beth said.

"Do you think it has to do with hidden secrets?" Kelsey's voice wavered.

Beth threw her hands up in the air. "Who knows what bats are in the belfry?"

"I have a feeling we'll uncover more than we bargained for." Kelsey replied.

"Keep focused on bringing your family back together."

"I will. Thanks for being a true friend and sticking by me."

Chapter 6

The next morning came early. Kelsey's cell phone began to jingle on the computer desk in her room. She threw a pillow over her head and groaned. *Beth, it better not be you waking me up this early to cancel.* She thought. "Hello?" Her voice was groggy.

"This is Abie Hall."

A panic ran threw her. She felt like a little girl about ready to get into trouble. "Y-Yes?" She asked with apprehension.

"We contacted Brody Bronson." Abie's voice was monotone and calm. "He agreed to meet the Princess Royale, but requested it be at a function so he wouldn't feel so pressured. Her Majesty is hosting a lunch this afternoon where the two will meet for the first time. He also asked you be there. We feel it might help to break the ice. The Queen wanted to honor you for making this event possible." Abie prided herself. There was no way Kelsey could uncover the secrets if she was at the lunch.

"I was supposed to meet my friend at ten so I'll have to cancel that."

"No, no. I insist you bring her with you."

"Really? You'd do that?" Maybe Miss Hall wasn't trying to sabotage the truth.

"Of course." Abie snickered to herself.

Kelsey heard the doorbell ring and the butler answer. She heard someone running up the stairs and knock on her bedroom door. She opened it half way. "Beth? What are you doing here so early?"

"We've got a busy day ahead of us. One of which is to figure out how we'll even get into the King's office."

"*Former* King." Kelsey sat down on the corner of her bed. "My Great Uncle Halton passed away last year. Now it is the Queen who is running the show herself."

"I'm sorry." Beth recalled the newspaper headlines. He had passed right before she met Kelsey at their church youth group.

"We weren't close, but it was still sad. Hopefully everything will change soon when I reveal the truth." Kelsey leapt off her bed with a spring in her step.

"Oh, and by the way, you seriously need to run a brush through that mop." Beth noticed the tangles that clumped in Kelsey's otherwise straight hair.

"I just woke up!" She threw a pillow at her. "Sit down for this." Kelsey took in a deep breath. "You are coming with me to the Palace."

"Yeah, I know. That's where the King keeps his things." Beth wondered if her friend hadn't been taking her vitamins lately.

"No. Abie called this morning and invited both of us to attend a luncheon they are hosting for the first meeting of Brody and the Princess!"

"Don't take this the wrong way, but why are they having us come?" Beth was reluctant to believe that Abie's invitation didn't hold ulterior motives.

"I'm the one who found him. Get this; she is honoring me at the event." Kelsey's eyes widened. "This could be the key to having a family."

"Do you really think just like that they will open their arms and welcome you right in?"

"I think they've realized I don't want the fame or fortunes. I'm helping the Princess because I genuinely want to and I want them."

Beth didn't have the heart to sink her dreams. She suspected Kelsey would have to do a lot more to win her family's affections.

She looked down at her worn, jean shorts, tennis shoes without socks and white tee shirt she borrowed from her brother. "I just have a hunch here, but I don't think this ensemble will be appropriate." She picked at her clothes.

"Thank goodness we're the same size then." Kelsey opened the French doors to her cedar lined closet. One side stored casual outfits and the other created a line of exquisite suits and dresses.

Beth fingered through them and picked out a strapless, red satin dress with a slit up the side. She put it against herself and raised an eyebrow at Kelsey.

"No." Kelsey brushed past her and pulled out a simple, buttercup yellow skirt with a small floral printed blouse and a pastel, green bolero jacket.

"That is not me." Beth grumbled.

"Don't worry. Everyone will be wearing the same type of clothes."

"Kels, I just got a thought. We're going to be at the palace anyhow, how about if we make a quick exit and locate the King's office?"

"As the guest of honor, they'll probably sit me at the head table or one close to it. How could I possibly get away without anyone noticing?"

"You're right - especially Abie Hall. We'll need a diversion."

"Oh, alright. I'll just bring some fire crackers from the last fourth of July." Kelsey's sarcasm tainted the air.

"I'm trying to help you." Beth put her hands on her hips. "If you think you can do this on your own then go ahead."

"Why do I need to keep going with this if they are willing to accept me now?"

Beth pursed her lips. "I've got to go home." Now that Kelsey felt wanted by her family, she didn't need her commoner friend anymore. She would be too busy with parties and find friends in her new peerage.

"Fine be that way!" Kelsey yelled back at her.

That afternoon, Kelsey arrived at the main ball room in the palace. She recognized some faces of her cousins, aunts and uncles, mostly from news prints. That is how she found out when someone was getting married or had a baby. She felt awkward in this circle and out of place. She mustered up her courage and became the charmer she needed to, to fit in.

I can do this by myself without Beth's help. I know these people better than she does. I bet Abie wasn't even covering anything up. She was probably just checking on me at the Queen's request. She justified.

Kelsey mingled amongst the crowned and sashayed with faux confidence and grace. Then, she saw them.

Brody had a casual suit jacket with khaki pants. His light, blue dress shirt accentuated his glowing sea blue eyes. He held her hand.

The Princess was wearing her blond wavy hair down and had a blush pink, floor length gown on. Her smile was infectious. She placed her other hand on his. She was elated. It showed in the creases of her eyes.

Princess Victoria whispered something in his ear, and his gorgeous, wide smile appeared again. The sight hit her hard, deep into the middle of her heart. It took her breath away.

How could I feel this way about someone I just met? Someone I don't know? She shook her head. *I must be confusing my emotions with something else.* She attempted to brush it off.

"Don't they make a beautiful couple?" A lady next to her sipped her tea.

"They would make equally beautiful offspring," commented another.

"I think it is a little premature for that." Kelsey placed her mini quiche on a table near her and went to find a seat.

Her name was elegantly scrolled on a place card at a round table near the main one. She didn't recognize the names of anyone she was sitting with.

She missed Beth. Her friend had put up with her schemes and wild ideas. Were the secrets worth investigating or were they all lies that she got caught up in? She noticed Abie's eyes from across the room. Kelsey gave a weak smile and received nothing in return but a blank face.

Shawn Scott, the Publicity Spokesman, grabbed the microphone. "We are pleased to have you all here." He shook his layered sandy blond hair. His deep chocolate eyes held sweetness. "You might see a new face in the crowd. Let me introduce the Earl of Atherton. He and the Princess have become great friends."

Kelsey waited for her introduction. Butterflies floated around in her belly.

The young Mr. Scott continued, "Enjoy the sit down lunch the Palace Chefs have prepared for you. Entertainment will follow on the back veranda." The Publicist put the microphone down and began to mingle.

No one knew who she was. No one cared. *This can't be happening. I do something nice for someone. I give up my chance for love and happiness and foolishly give up my friendship with Beth… for what?* The anger welled inside her like a bubbling pool of lava. How could she have been so deceived?

I will find out what they are hiding and when I do, they'll take notice. She heard another voice in her head. *I can't do this out of revenge. My motives need to be right and for the same reasons why I started looking into this in the first place.* She concluded. *I might not have Beth's help right now, but I've got to pull my self-confidence together so that I can do this.*

She excused herself from the table and pretended to go into the ladies' room across the hall. She peered out of the door to make sure Abie's glaring eyes were not upon her and slipped back down the corridor to find the Kings office. Guards were at every entrance including the elevators and stairways. Doubts filled her mind, subduing her self belief.

Lord God, please help me to reveal the truth. Forgive me for not putting you first in my life lately. You are always my God and the One I turn to. Keep me safe and help Beth to know I'm sorry until I can tell her face to face.

The guard blocking the stairs held his walkie-talkie up to his ear. It echoed static off the tile walls. "There is a water main break at the entrance of the palace. All of the gates keep opening and closing. It is threatening to compromise the safety of the guests. You are needed immediately!"

"Coming." He answered back, and left his post.

She looked behind her and quietly snuck up the stairs. "At least Abie doesn't know where I need to go next." She whispered to herself. Another guard ran down the hall of the fourth floor responding to the immediate need of the hay wired gates.

Kelsey gathered her courage and asked God to lead her in the right direction. The first room she can across was filled with instruments and the next had several plants and flowers. She got to the last room and saw filled book cases, three desks, and a large, wooden chest with two drawers at the bottom. She immediately snuck into what she concluded as the office.

Kelsey pulled at the locked drawers and remembered what Beth had suggested the last time they needed to open one. She removed a bobby pin from her hair and popped the seal. She quickly riffled through mounds of envelopes and old papers. The dates on them kept getting older the further down she went. Then, what she saw next, rattled her. She held several large papers half completed.

She pulled them out and placed them on the desk to take a closer look. She saw the same date of Graham's birth written by hand, along with his name, Duke Dane and Duchess in quivering letters. Then she saw a mistake in the spelling of Graham's name. She turned to the next paper. It was more complete with the right spelling and a steadier hand. The following papers revealed a marriage certificate.

The church's names were different on the two partly scribed renditions. *It's as if someone were forging them, trying to get it right!* Kelsey postulated. *Why would the King have their half-written documents? How do I prove this and what would it tell me?*

She needed to see copies of several birth and marriage certificates from that time period to compare them. She pulled out her camera and took several pictures of each paper.

Was the marriage real? If they needed to fake a birth, where did the baby come from? Now that I know the name of the Duchess, I can research her, too. Kelsey's head was swamped with more questions than when she began. The fuel of these new clues added to her intention to see this mystery to the end.

She gently closed the drawer and slipped her camera into her skirt pocket. Kelsey peaked out of the doorway into the empty hall, and ran for the stairs. She rejoined the exuberant party guests who had migrated to the veranda. A magician was entertaining a small crowd on the left and the same harpist that was at the Duke's castle was playing on the right while people quietly socialized in front of the instrument.

She felt a hand on her back and quickly turned around. It was Brody.

"Having a good time?" Brody asked, flashing his shiny teeth.

"Sure. I bet *you* are. Was she all you could have dreamed?"

"Who?" Brody's forehead wrinkled.

"The Princess." Kelsey knitted her brows together in surprise.

"Oh, her. Well yeah, if that's your type."

"How could she not be?"

"Sometimes guys want someone more like themselves. Someone they can easily laugh with and be down to earth."

Kelsey fiddled with the cuff of her sleeve. "Isn't she all of that?

"I think you hold her on a higher pedestal than most people. Don't get me wrong, she is kind. There just isn't any spark."

"Sparks are great." She said, getting lost in his eyes for a moment. "I mean, if I knew what the feeling of being in love was like, which I don't." She looked away

"That's too bad. It's an amazing emotion, like a rush of adrenaline." He calmly replied and walked away.

A moment later, her cell phone buzzed.

"Hello?"

"Hi again." Brody's deep voice startled her.

She turned in every direction and saw him standing a hundred yards away. He had one hand in his pant pocket and waved at her with the other. She giggled. "You were just here. Why are you calling me? And how did you get my cell phone number?"

"Like it was that hard? I have connections you know."

"Well, don't let it go to your head. Knowing the Royal Family gets you a lot of Places." She brushed a piece of hair out of her face. "This is what I was trying to explain to you in the garden. You could do so much with your career if you married the Princess. You would have monetary support and the buy-in of the community."

"There is so much more to life. Kelsey, what if you could have a career *and* true love?"

She remained silent on the other end not knowing how to reply.

"I called you because I just received notice that Beth is trying to get into the palace but can't seem to get past the immense amount of guards trying to control the open gates. She asked for you, but no one knew where you were at."

"Thanks. I'll go get her." She bolted toward the main entrance and saw Beth attempting to convince one of the staff to let her through. Kelsey came up behind the man. "It's alright. I know her. She's my best friend." She gave Beth a hug. "I'm so sorry." Kelsey sighed. "I was just under so much pressure."

Beth smiled and hugged her back. "So, can I come in?"

"No." Then she turned to the guard, "we have other places to go." She grabbed Beth by her elbow. "I'll explain in the car. Where are you parked by the way?"

Beth pointed to her beat up, orange truck. "I don't think you've ever ridden in this, have you?"

"That would be a big, no." Kelsey's door squeaked on the passenger side and she hopped up into the black, ripped up seat. "How did that happen?" She nervously pointed to the slash marks.

Beth cackled. "I had to take my German Sheppard to the vet and he wasn't too keen on the idea." She put the key in the ignition and started the engine. She saw Abie Hall out of the corner of her eye at the gates. Beth shoved Kelsey's head down.

"What are you doing?" Kelsey asked.

Beth slouched down. "It's Abie. You don't want her to see you leave. You never know if she'd have you followed."

"Good thinking." Kelsey's words came out muffled from her cramped position.

Beth shifted gears. "So where should I start driving? I kind of thought we needed to search the palace."

"Already did and we are headed toward the registrar's office." She updated Beth on her recent find and idea to compare the documents to real ones from that time period. "We might even be able to find a census record or something with the Duchess's name or information so we know who she is."

Chapter 7

They approached the receptionist at the registrar's office. "Ma'am, where could we find documents from the early 1600's?" Kelsey inquired.

The woman looked up at the girls over her bright, red framed bifocals and motioned for the girls to follow her without a word.

She took them to the lowest level of the building and into the archives room. The gray, cement walls smelled of must.

"Why do they always keep the interesting things in basements?" Kelsey giggled.

"That is a good question." The secretary added. She knelt down smoothing her pencil skirt and examined the thick, brown books with dates scrolled on the binders. She pulled one out and laid it on a nearby oak table with 1970's looking, plastic blue seats surround it. "Will that be all you need help with?"

The girls nodded and she disappeared up the stairs. Kelsey pulled out her camera and brought up the first shot she had taken.

Meanwhile, Beth had flipped to the area with the marriage certificates. They both looked closely at the photo and back at the paper.

"They look so similar." Beth remarked.

Kelsey examined it closer. "Look at this." She pointed to the top of the paper where the words spelled out 'Marriage

Certificate' in a half arc shape with the first letters of each word capitalized.

Careful attention was paid to the centering of it. She showed Beth the picture she took. The photo revealed only the 'M' in marriage was capitalized, not the 'C' of the next word. It was not as centered as the document they were viewing in the book.

Beth flipped through several of them and they all looked the same, but the photo still had minute differences. "I bet the King's seal was all the registrar looked at."

"They would not have questioned him." Kelsey postulated.

"True."

They found the same small mistakes with Graham's birth certificate. Then, Kelsey saw something that made her heart stop.

"Are you alright?" Beth reacted to the look on her friend's face.

"No." She sat stunned. "Here." She turned the book closer to her friend.

Beth's eye's slowly read a separate birth certificate that showed a twin birth. One girl named Flora and one boy named Graham. They were born to Azuriah Telton. The father's name was left out.

"Both Grahams were born on the same day. How unique is that, especially with the connection to Azuriah?" Beth commented.

"It has to be the same person." Kelsey walked back over to the book of the late 1600s.

"What are you doing? Don't you want to lament on this for a second?"

"I've got a hunch." Kelsey dropped the book with a thud on the table and rolled her eyes upward trying to calculate in her head. She flipped through all the birth certificates of that time period. "Just as I thought; there's nothing on file for the Duke's wife."

"Maybe she wasn't born around here." Beth didn't want to complicate matters but felt the options had to be heard.

"I thought about that, but all the rumors talk of her being born to a wealthy family from this countryside. They say no one had heard of her because their family was reclusive." Kelsey sighed. "I don't think she ever existed."

"Why would the Duke make her up when he could have married Azuriah?" Beth wondered.

"Azuriah had to have had these twins with someone. She might have gone off with another man." Kelsey leaned on the desk with both arms and let the weight of her body release.

"I just can't imagine that." Beth sat down in exhaustion. "Why had Duke Dane kept the letters she had sent him? Wouldn't that have angered him since he was in love with her?"

"If we stay on this trail, we'll eventually figure it out. I want to have sufficient evidence and not just jump to conclusions or no one will ever believe us." Kelsey put the camera back in her purse.

"Who are you going to tell, the press, the Queen, the public?" Beth stood up. "Do you know what might happen if it was proved that Graham was not Duke Dane's?"

Kelsey stared blankly at Beth with wide eyes.

"It could very well mean the fall of the royal family." A stunned silence followed Beth's words. "That is probably why Abie Hall has been hot on our trail and trying to get in between you and the truth. We have to stop here."

"No. This can't be right. It doesn't make sense." Kelsey said.

"Not a whole lot of things do in this world."

"I know, but this is different." She turned to Beth with a look of determination. "You trust me, right?"

"Of course, but…"

"No buts," Kelsey uttered through pursed lips. "We need to uncover this, then I'll figure out if I keep silent or not."

"To be honest, I'm scared of the repercussions. This involves the whole country, not just you."

"Yes, it does. That is why I will determine if I need to reveal it or not when we find out the whole story."

Beth inhaled a long, deep breath and slowly let it out. "If you decide to go public with what we find, will you promise to keep my name out of this?"

"Yes. I am the one who started this fiasco. I just feel blessed that you are helping me." Kelsey gave a weak smile.

"Okay, I'll continue on with you, but if this starts getting dangerous, I'm pulling out and you will have to finish this alone." Beth stood firm.

"Deal." They shook hands.

Kelsey's phone began to ring. She looked at the caller id. It read, Abie Hall. "What does she want now? I bet she saw I wasn't around anymore."

"I'm surprised your cell works in this basement." Beth shrugged and eavesdropped on the conversation.

"Kelsey, we want you to meet us in the main office of the palace in ten minutes." Abie requested.

"A-Alright." She replied apprehensively.

"Abie must think I'm still at the luncheon since she asked to meet with me so quickly. How fast can your truck go?"

Beth stared at her with a frown. "If I take a few short cuts, it could happen."

They ran to the truck and torn out of the parking lot. A few bumpy roads later, the vehicle came to a stop at a wooded area near the side of the palace. Kelsey flung her heels off and ran like mad.

Finally! They are going to acknowledge me for setting up the Princess. I can't wait to speak to my Great Aunt even though I still call her Queen.

She stopped in front of the room, wiped the sweat from her forehead, pinned her hair back more securely and jumped into her shoes.

She entered the office with grace and ease. Abie came out from behind the desk to shake her hand, before retreating back to her black, leather chair.

"I would like to personally congratulate you on finding a good match for the Princess Royale. The Queen is so thrilled and will continue to entrust you with other requests as they arise." She stated with a look of satisfaction on her face.

"You mean she's not coming?"

"No. Why would she when it is something I can do for her?"

"Oh, I don't know, because she is my relative?" Kelsey clenched her fists.

"That is not dignified behavior. Maybe that is why she didn't come." Abie's ruthless comment cut deep into Kelsey's soul.

Abie might be the barrier preventing me from bonding with my family, but I'm so close to finding out the truth. This could alter Abie's position so fast, her head will spin. If only she knew that I hold cards too, but I must pretend she has the upper hand right now or I may never be able to get the truth or my family back.

Kelsey left the room with her respect intact.

Chapter 8

Princess Victoria and the Earl of Atherton strolled along the walking paths at the back of the palace with two body guards trailing fifty yards behind them.

"Everyone is so happy we've met." Brody commented with resistance in his tone.

Victoria's slender frame slumped ever so slightly. She hated to admit it, but had to tell him her feelings. "May I call you Brody?"

"I would be happy if you did." He took pleasure in the reduced formalities.

They walked a little further down the path, both looking in opposite directions trying to avoid the inevitable. Brody motioned for the two to sit on a wooden bench.

"All this must be overwhelming." She hinted to Brody.

"I would be lying if I didn't say a little. I'm used to some of this, being an Earl and all, but the romantic set up is new to me."

"Me too."

"You are a lovely girl." He tried to begin.

"And you're lovely too." She could sense what he was about to say and knew it would be difficult to tell a princess. "Do you see yourself with me in the future?"

Brody hesitated. "I don't think you will have a problem finding suitors who are interested in living this life."

She started laughing.

"What?" He began to chuckle a little at her behavior.

"Oh, thank God. I thought we'd have more strange moments before we figured out that we feel the exact same way about each other."

"You mean that we like each other as friends but there is no chemistry," Brody said.

"Precisely!" She smiled and giggled some more.

"Do you know Kelsey Dane, the girl who got us together?" He asked.

"I don't know her but we've crossed paths at family functions," Princess Victoria admitted.

"She is the one my heart belongs to." He confessed.

"I'm secretly in love with our family's Publicist, Shawn Scott!"

"Do you think we could help one another?" He held his hopes high.

"I'm curious to hear how this one is going to be accomplished."

Brody whispered in her ear.

Kelsey wallowed in her own self pity while trying to escape the whole charade. She wanted to get away from it all and saw a path way down by a stream. She walked looking up at the clouds and trees around her. The breeze glided across her face and she felt free for a second.

She looked ahead of her and stopped. Brody and the Princess were giggling and whispering sweet nothings into each other's ears. She fumed. *He was just flirting with me on the veranda. Were his words all lies?* It wasn't so much that they were getting along – that was her doing. She had found him for the Princess. He was to be Victoria's, alone. What got to her were his lies.

I thought he cared for me during that instant we were talking. He made it seem like he didn't love the Princess, but could that have changed? She turned away and plopped down by the water's edge.

"Isn't that Kelsey over there?" The Princess pointed from the bench they were conversing on.

He squinted against the sun's rays and placed his hand over his eyes. "Yes, it is." He was surprised. "Do you mind if I go and speak with her?"

"Go get her." Princess Victoria felt pleased with their arrangement in the quest to get their true loves.

He slowly approached Kelsey as not to scare her away.

She looked up at him and turned her eyes back to the river.

"You look so sad." He read her face.

"Things aren't going exactly as planned." She hugged her knees.

"They rarely do."

"That is what Beth keeps telling me. One of these days I'm going to realize it."

He laughed. "May I join you?"

She nodded.

The grass felt soft below him as he sat beside her.

"Anything I can help with?"

"Unfortunately it is something I have to do myself." She gave a weak smile at his offer. "I see you and the Princess were getting along better than you had thought you would."

"Yeah, imagine that. It's the beginning of a good friendship, but there isn't any chemistry between us."

"It will come."

"I doubt it. We are both in love with different people."

Kelsey jerked her head toward his. "Who?"

"Well, I promised not to reveal hers, but I will tell you who I like if you promise not to tell anyone." He placed his fingers gently on her chin and moved his mouth closer to hers.

She felt like she were floating and went along with his movements. Then her brain reminded her she was still in reality. She placed her hand on his chest and pushed her head away from his, millimeters before their lips touched.

"No. You don't realize what you are doing! The Princess is right there." Kelsey pointed. "She is who you should be with. Gosh, could you imagine what would happen to us if the Royal Court found out I stole the guy meant for the Princess Royale. We'd be ostracized!"

"So?"

"How does that not affect you? Do you think your family would approve of your actions?" She paused. "I'm a commoner." Her chin quivered. She took a deep breath and continued. "You are *way* above my peerage."

"Don't you think I know what I'm doing?" His eyes firmly locked into hers. "Here you say you are trying so hard to get your family together, but did you ever think about the family you could create?"

He tempted her mind with visions of her soul mate and children running happily through the grass on a hillside picnic.

She took his hand in both of hers trying to reason with him. "You are too great a person not the marry her."

"How sane is that to keep two people apart who love each other? You would give that up just so that your family can give you a pat on the back and continue in their old ways?" His anger flamed.

She was taken aback by the intensity of his emotions.

"Tell me you don't love me too?" Brody's voice deepened.

She didn't know how to react. "You deserve a better life than you'd have with me."

"You are right, Kelsey. We can't be together because you need to love yourself before you could love me." He stormed off toward the Princess.

Kelsey sat in shock fighting an impulsive reaction to go after him and tell him that he is her true love.

Chapter 9

The following day Kelsey awoke with a heavy heart. Her guilt plagued her from the last conversation she had with Brody. She had to get away – a place where she could think and just be.

They had first met in the west garden where Duke Dane and Azuriah would hide their love from the world. She decided to go back there. It was a day that few people skirted away from town. She should have enough privacy.

Kelsey jumped into her convertible and took the long way through the country side to the Duke's castle. The intermittent shade from the trees she drove by appeared like the flicker of an old black and white movie. A story where in the end, the lovers reunite.

After a few hours of driving, she turned down the long, gravel driveway to the castle. The sunlight was shining upon it. The grass and shrubbery was neatly trimmed and only Mrs. Short's car was there.

She opened the large, wooden door and saw the historian typing at her desk. They exchanged waves. She continued through the mansion and out the back toward the garden. Freshly bloomed flowers caressed her senses. She left her shoes by the gate and stepped onto the spongy moss that wound its way through the beauty.

Kelsey secretly hoped Brody would be there. In her mind's eye, he would look up at her with that fantastic smile, race to her and hold her in his arms in a passionate embrace ending in a kiss. It was not meant to be and she was the only one there. She tried to capture his essence and remember his smell.

She examined the leaves of the different plants and held them in the palm of her hand, tracing their veins with her fingers. After reminiscing in the garden, she took herself back to the castle to casually wander. She wanted to get lost into another world- a world where the righteousness of love conquered societal rules.

Kelsey found herself looking into a room that appeared to be the Duke's bedchamber. Each step seemed to transport her back in time. Then, she saw a hand carved box setting silently on a vanity. What secrets must it have kept? She decided to open it to see if it played a melody. The hinges creaked from age. There was nothing inside. *Of course there was nothing. Abie mentioned she scoured the place for artifacts to display in the exhibit room.*

The box was lined with a patterned, velvety fabric. She was about to close the box when she noticed a piece of material had come loose from its tack. She gently tugged at it. It pulled back to reveal a round, ivory container that had been hidden between the top of the box and lining. She removed it and twisted the lid off. Inside was a long, brown curl tied with a faded pink ribbon.

Was this a lock of Azuriah's hair? Then it hit her. Beth's uncle Clark worked at the crime lab. If she took this to him, would he be able to link it to her? Could she find something to prove Graham was hers? She knew if she could confirm those things, she might also be able to figure out who the father was. This might be the key that tied her research together.

Kelsey slipped the hair inside its container into her purse and nonchalantly strolled past Mrs. Short and back to her car. She had to get over to Beth's house. She attempted several phone calls on the way to her home but only got her voice mail.

The next call went through. "Beth, I've been desperately trying to get a hold of you. Where have you been?"

"In the shower. What's so urgent?"

"I had a lot on my mind, so I decided to go up to the castle to get away and think."

"Did all this thinking have to do with Brody?" Beth hoped she would tell her there was a change in their relationship.

"Yes, but listen to me! I found a lock of hair that might be Azuriah's." Kelsey's mind was racing.

"What? Now how did that happen?"

"It's not important right now. This is what I need you to do. Call your uncle who works at the crime lab. See if he can test our sample." Kelsey adjusted her sun glasses. "We also need to know how he could genetically link a deceased mother, father and their children."

"Alright, it's one o' clock now so he should be back from lunch. How much should I tell him?"

"Just enough for him to answer our questions." Kelsey stopped at a cross roads and looked both ways. "I'll be back in town in about an hour and a half. Call me with what your uncle says and maybe I could meet you at the lab."

It seemed to take forever before Beth called her back.

"What did you find out?" Kelsey asked.

"Well, you're not going to like this." Beth informed.

"He can't test the sample?"

"Oh no, he can test it," Beth remarked.

"Then what's the problem?" Kelsey asked.

"He said he would need samples from the others to determine a match." Beth sighed at the complexity of the situation.

"H-How do we do that?"

"That is the tough part. He said the bodies would have to be exhumed. He would need a sample of their teeth if possible."

"There is no way I'm going to do that!" Kelsey shuddered. "Number one, it's against the law; number two it is unethical for me; and number three, that is just plain gross!"

"There is something else you forgot to include." Beth's concern grew. "Once he gets the paper work filed and if he is allowed to go ahead with the exhumation, Graham's identity will be revealed and the press will be all over it."

"Don't we have the option of making it public knowledge?" Kelsey asked.

"No. If Graham is not the son of Duke Rupert Dane, then you have to be prepared for the consequences," Beth said.

"So what if he was adopted? He's still his son," Kelsey attempted to reconcile.

"The royal family is only reigning because there is a direct lineage to the first King and Queen of the country. Our government is set up that way." Beth grabbed her brush and started combing her hair in the mirror. "They could change that in the future, but there is no guarantee.

"So what you are saying is that I would have to be prepared to live with the fact that I found reason to dethrone the royal family?" Kelsey approached a stop light and slammed on her breaks before nearly missing a car coming in the opposite direction.

"Basically." Beth winced.

"I'm sure that Parliament would decide righteously." Kelsey's heart beat wildly after almost colliding with the other vehicle.

"That is the other issue. God is the only righteous one. People don't always do what is correct," Beth said.

Kelsey drove around a bend. "Can you and your uncle give me time to think about this before he proceeds?"

"Of course." Beth empathized. "There is a loop hole for my uncle to be allowed to do an exhumation."

"Do I want to hear this?"

"If he were doing a doctoral thesis researching the Duke and his descendants, then he would most likely get permission from the authorities to study their remains, especially since they have never been examined before."

"Wow." Kelsey stared wide eyed onto the road in front her.

"I know. What I can't believe is that he can't wait to do it."

"You have got to be kidding me!"

"He is a huge history buff. There is only one thing holding him back. He needs to apply for his doctorate, get admitted and sign up for classes. He'll also have to get permission from the lab to conduct this study there." Beth stated.

"How long would that take?"

"Roughly three months."

"Considering the alternative, which is nothing, it sounds as if that is the only option. I'll try to make a decision soon as to whether the outcome is something that my family and I could handle." Kelsey concluded.

"You know, this three month break could give you the opportunity to get to know Brody better," Beth teased.

"Oh, stop. He and the Princess are suited for each other. They just don't know it yet." Kelsey sighed.

"Promise me I can be your Maid of Honor?"

A nervous laugh escaped her. "For sure, just don't hold your breath for that to be anytime soon. Mr. Right hasn't swept me off my feet yet."

Chapter 10

That afternoon, Kelsey arrived at Beth's house.

"I was just about to call the search party." Beth walked into her bedroom and turned on the radio.

"Traffic was terrible."

"Christina called from our church youth group. They need more volunteers to visit the sick at the hospital tonight. There's a get together at four o'clock to put the gift baskets together," Beth said.

"I need to call Brody to apologize, so I might as well ask him to come while we're on the phone." Kelsey's heart leapt out of her chest at the thought.

Beth glanced at her with knowing eyes.

Kelsey dialed his number. He picked up immediately.

"That was quick." She replied.

"I saw your name on the caller I.D." He said.

"I'm sorry for making you upset at the luncheon." Adrenaline pulsed through her veins.

"I'm over it."

Kelsey hesitated. "For what it's worth, I didn't do it intentionally."

"Thanks. Does that mean you changed your mind?" Brody's desires were tangible.

"I'm calling to invite you to come with me tonight. My friends from church are making up gifts for the patients in the hospital."

Finally, he felt he was breaking down her walls. "Yeah, I'll be there."

Kelsey gave him directions. "Call Princess Victoria for me to see if she can make it."

It was too late. He had already committed. If he had known her motives were only to get him and the Princess together, he would have turned Kelsey down.

That night Beth and Kelsey sat and listened to the Youth Director in the church's gymnasium. "I don't know how we pulled this off at such short notice. We're not only visiting with the sick, but able to give them inspirational gifts from the heart."

"What is that, some kind of fuzzy stuffed animal?" Kelsey examined one of the soft objects Beth had brought.

"I crocheted chenille socks and put little grippies on the bottom. Who doesn't like those, am I right?" Beth asked.

Brody walked in through a side door. Princess Victoria and Shawn Scott trailed behind him holding hands.

Kelsey's jaw dropped.

"This is just a guess, but I'm thinking that its clear Brody and Victoria will not be dating." Beth whispered. She raised her hand for the three to come sit with them.

Victoria pushed her long hair behind her shoulder. "Here's a bunch of balloons." She tossed them on the table.

Brody took a seat next to Beth. "Hey guys; my birthday's this weekend and my parents are throwing me a party at our cottage. Who can come?"

"I'm not sure what I have going on." Kelsey muttered.

"I happen to know she is free." Beth interjected.

The rest confirmed they would be there.

The Director handed out baskets for everyone to fill with the things they had brought or made. They followed each other in their cars to the hospital.

The group walked to a half circle desk. The Nurse Manager walked out from behind. "I take it you are the cheer squad?" She led them just outside of a room. "The first patient you'll be seeing is Zach. He is an eight year old boy with leukemia. He is especially happy today because he just found out his body is healing and the cancer is going away."

Kelsey walked in first. The little boy's face lit up when he saw the cake she was carrying. "I hear you have great news."

"Yeah," He sat up in bed. "I'm getting out of here in another few days. What have you got?" He noticed the full basket.

Victoria tied some balloons to the side of his bed, and Brody handed him some purple roses.

Kelsey glanced over at Brody who gave her a warm smile. She sat next to the boy and read him an adventure story. Brody's heart softened.

"What's that?" Zach pointed to an electronic box Shawn carried.

"Are you a good singer?" Shawn knelt down next to the hospital bed.

"I'm terrible at it, but its fun." Zach replied.

Shawn had him pick from a long list of nineteen fifties songs.

"What if we get in trouble?" His eyes widened.

"Do you really think they'll kick us out?" Shawn started off loud and the others joined in off key.

The nurses heard the commotion. "Should we say something?" One of them asked the other.

"No, they are just helping make our jobs easier. We are in charge of getting them better. They always say laughter is the best medicine."

The group went on to visit a woman who had surgery on her appendix and an elderly man with swollen joints. All of the patient's vitals were up by the end of their stay.

The group started to leave down the hall way.

Kelsey pulled Brody aside. "I've been working on self acceptance and understanding that each person is more precious than the universe to God. Jesus died for every single one of us, so we could be with Him in Heaven. I'm beginning to see that I'm worthy of being loved in return. Thanks for helping me realize what I needed to rediscover in order to love others as they should be loved."

He pulled her into a bear hug and rested his chin on her head. "We all have our flaws. I don't want to tell you what mine are. It might drive you away!" He joked.

"I bite my nails." She admitted.

He paused before coming clean with it. "I'm hopelessly unorganized."

"I won't hold it against you." She laughed.

Chapter 11

That same day at the Palace, Queen Marabel sat in her velvet, ornately carved chair and sipped her green tea. Abie tapped on the open door with the back of her knuckles to announce her presence.

"You wanted more crème for your drink?" Abie offered.

"Yes, and please sit down. What new information do you have on Kelsey? Have you managed to way lay her?"

"Kelsey and her friend Beth are determined to uncover the secret. Any attempts to stop them have proved futile."

"How so?"

"I did as you asked and went to the castle to supervise her. I stayed behind the group so no one would notice me." Fear soared into her body hoping she would not let the Queen down. "When I approached the kitchen, I spotted Mrs. McCreedy and the girls slip into the pantry."

"Lynn McCreedy is a gossip!" Her Majesty angrily placed her tea cup loudly upon its saucer almost cracking it.

"Don't worry, I sent her home for the day. I also told her she was not allowed to speak to Kelsey or Beth anymore."

The Queen groaned with thankfulness.

"I tried to keep Kelsey's mind off of her quest by instructing her to find an eligible bachelor for your daughter."

"Is *that* where the Earl of Atherton came from?"

"Yes, Your Highness." She replied, trying to sense if their pairing pleased the Queen.

"I like him." She bobbed her head. "Now continue."

"I later found them snooping around Duke Dane's study. I ushered them out and saw they had nothing in their hands."

"Thank God! What were they looking for?" The Queen arched one brow.

"I don't know. They even went so far as to poke around the graveyard and church after dusk!"

"We must nip this in the bud," Her Majesty demanded.

"I called the caretaker and sent him out immediately to shoo them away."

"Since they haven't found anything that you know of, I believe we are safe. They are probably just bored little girls who are looking for adventure. They have no idea what they are getting into," the Queen spoke in a hushed tone.

"The last I checked, she had stopped her silliness and continued her normal routine."

"Good. Keep a close eye on her. You may leave now Miss Hall."

Her Majesty thought back to the time when the secret was revealed to her by King Halton Dane's mother. She was twenty two when Halton, then a Prince, proposed marriage. They wed the next year and she was welcomed into the close family unit as Princess.

The Queen took her into the chapel to kneel in prayer. They both prayed separately for awhile, then, her mother-in-law asked her to keep her eyes closed and her hands together. "Since you are now in a royal position and may acquire my title someday, I feel the time is right to tell you. This tale must not escape your lips or the crown may fall."

Princess Marabel declared her utmost secrecy in front of God.

Her mother-in-law began to retell of the King's illness and having to turn the thrown over to Duke Dane. The Duke was not expected to produce children. "We are from the lineage of a child he adopted and named Graham. He refused to marry anyone other than a woman named Azuriah whom was a commoner. So, the King forged a marriage to a fake person and also forged Graham's birth certificate. If this is found out, we will be dethroned unless Parliament changes the laws."

Marabel remembered how the story had gripped her and how thankful she was to have been able to keep her love with Halton since she had been in the high peerage of society. She was not about to let the story leak out after it had been guarded for centuries. She had, had Miss Hall excavate the property five years back to ensure nothing was left for anyone to discover.

Chapter 12

Kelsey and Beth arrived at the Bronson's two story cottage over grown on the corners with ivy. Moss covered the roofs shingles which grew in abundance from the shade of the forest.

Brody came out to greet them.

"How was the drive?" He hugged Kelsey and smiled at Beth.

"It was beautiful driving through the hills and country side." Kelsey placed her arms around his waist linking her hands together behind him.

Beth popped the trunk to get their luggage.

"Let me do that." He hoisted their suitcases with ease. "I'll show you where the girls will be sleeping, then give you the tour." He led them into the main house and down to the walk out basement.

"Oh my goodness!" Beth glanced around the room at the pool table, hot tub and shuffle board.

"My parents love to entertain." Brody responded.

"I can see why." Kelsey looked out the French doors onto the three tiered patio surrounded by trees.

"Come on, I'll show you around outside." Brody took them onto the patio and down a few brick steps. "We have a private lake over here." He pointed to the left. "It isn't very large, but it is big enough to wakeboard."

Two buildings that looked like smaller versions of the cottage, stood near the edge of the water. "What are those?" Beth inquired.

"One is the boat house where we store all the beach toys, chairs and water crafts. The other is the guest house where the guys will be staying tonight."

Kelsey could see a small waterfall spilling into a babbling brook which led to the lake. "Where is the rest of the party?"

They heard a car's engine getting closer. "Sounds like they're here," Brody said.

They ran up to the front of the house to meet Victoria and Shawn. "You guys can't tell the Queen I'm here. I told her I was at an educational seminar on genetics."

"Victoria breeds poodles for show." Shawn chuckled.

"Isn't it dangerous going around without your body guards?" Beth asked.

"No one followed us. The paparazzi are waiting for me to show up at the college. Plus, Shawn will protect me."

"Yeah, I borrowed a bullet proof vest just in case it gets ugly." He joked.

Brody showed them to their sleeping quarters and then joined the group on the patio for a buffet lunch. Two rectangular tables covered in white linens held silver warming trays with sweet potatoes, corn, green beans and bar-be-cued chicken.

"I can't imagine what they serve for dinner!" Beth whispered to Shawn.

"No kidding."

Beth put her plate down and walked over to Brody who was waiting last in line. "Did you ask her yet?"

"I'm too nervous." Brody admitted.

"You told me after we all left the hospital that you would ask her to be your girlfriend."

"I'm scared of being rejected. She has pushed me away for so long. She seems comfortable with me now and we're starting to get closer. I don't want to be hasty about it if she isn't ready."

"How are you going to know unless you ask?" Beth prodded.

"That is what I'm afraid of. I may only get one opportunity. If I don't time it right, she might shut me out."

"Do you want me to talk to her about the subject and see how responsive she is?"

"That would take so much pressure off." Brody patted her on the back.

After lunch, Victoria and Shawn decided to take a stab at fishing and Brody revved up the inboard speed boat at the dock.

Kelsey sat in the back as a spotter and Beth bobbed in the water with skis on. Kelsey threw her the rope. She noticed a guy about their age walking on the dock toward them. His hair was as dark and shiny as night. He had an olive complexion and walked with a limp. "Who is that?"

Brody looked up. "Demitri! Hey, what happened to your leg?"

"I hurt it in a skate boarding competition. I let my nerves get to me and screwed up a trick."

Kelsey saw Beth's eyes bulging out of her head at the site of this guy. He was really cute but she had to wonder if something else wasn't wrong. "Beth, are you alright?"

She nodded and improvised a grin.

"Get in the boat. We were just about to take my friend skiing." Brody said.

He leapt in and sat in the back near Kelsey.

Brody introduced Demitri to everyone.

"I already know Beth," Demitri said in a coquettish facade.

Kelsey cocked her head with pinched brows.

"She is my ex girlfriend." He replied to her silent question.

Later in the day, the sun began to fade into the horizon. Brody's parents pulled up in their red, Lamborghini. The group of friends walked up the hill to the house to change out of their swim suites.

Brody introduced Kelsey to his mom and dad. His mother had a tall, medium built frame and strawberry blonde hair to her shoulders. His father was a little shorter and pudgier with a ring of silver hair around his head.

"We are so delighted to meet you Kelsey. Are you all having fun?" His mother asked.

"Yes! Brody taught me how to ski and Princess Victoria was fishing with the Palace Publicist." Kelsey's hands were sweaty and shook.

"What would make a great evening is an old fashioned camp fire. I'll get some kindling and light it for you guys," his dad offered.

"Dear, why don't you have the staff set up the outdoor movie screen?" Mrs. Bronson turned to her husband.

"Great idea. What are your favorite shows Kelsey? I'll check to see if we have them."

"Hum. I'd have to say *The Notebook* by Nicholas Sparks, thank you."

His parents retreated into the house.

"What do you think of them?" Brody poked Kelsey's side.

Kelsey giggled, "Love them! But did they like me?"

"My parents are never that accommodating unless they approve of my friends."

"I may have good breeding, but they know I'm only in a peerage by distant relation." *I wonder what they'll think when the truth comes out. I might not even have royal ties*, she thought.

"It won't matter to them. They have always told me they support what makes me happy."

Kelsey couldn't help but wonder if they would still feel that way when the lab results were revealed.

The bon fire spanned six feet in a circle. The staff had set up teak wood benches and Adirondack chairs. Long metal poles were given out for roasting marsh mellows. The night had set and fireflies scattered their glow all around them. After stuffing themselves with s'mores and soda, they turned their chairs around to watch the movie. His parents brought out warmed blankets for them.

Brody and Kelsey cuddled next to each other and Beth pleaded with Victoria to sit in between her and Shawn so she wouldn't get stuck sitting next to Demitri.

Kelsey was dying to ask her what had happened with her and her ex. She decided to wait until they went back to their separate quarters for the night before having some serious girl talk. She focused her attention on Brody.

He started fidgeting. He kept opening his mouth to speak and then sighed.

"Is there something on your mind?" She asked.

He took a deep breath. "I was going to wait a little longer, but it feels like the time is right. I pray you're open to it. If not, just promise me you won't shut our friendship down. I don't want things to get weird between us."

She hesitated. "Gosh, you're scaring me. I can't imagine anything would change us being friends."

He looked up to Heaven searching for guidance from God. He turned to her. "I want to formally ask you if you would be my girlfriend?" He winced, waiting for a rejection.

"Is that all?" Kelsey leaned back in her chair. "I have to say, you really spooked me."

"Well?" Brody questioned.

"Can I tell you the answer before we leave tomorrow?" She didn't want to rush into any decision and mess things up between them.

"Sure." He didn't know how to handle what she said so he played it cool the rest of the night.

The movie ended and they all helped clean up the area and fold the blankets into a neat pile before going their separate ways.

The girls took turns in the two basement bathrooms. Kelsey finished brushing her teeth and snuggled into her sleeping bag. She propped herself on her elbows. "Beth, are you going to tell us about Demitri?"

"There is not much to divulge. We met at design school a few years ago when I first moved to this country. We began dating right away but all he wanted to do was skate board all the time. He thought he was the best one out there and when he wouldn't get first place, he'd throw a tantrum. That is when I called it quits."

"That's too bad. I wonder if he is still like that. People change all the time." Kelsey said.

"And some don't." Beth rolled her eyes. "I'm not going above and beyond to figure that out. If we frequented the same places then I'd have the opportunity to see if he has, but I doubt we'll see each other again." She rolled her black curls into a bun. "It looked like you and Brody were getting along well."

"He asked me to be his girlfriend."

"Amen!" Beth shouted. "It took him long enough. He has wanted to ask you that for so long but couldn't get up the courage."

"Really? That is so cute."Kelsey gleamed.

Victoria paused from washing her face. "What are you going to tell him?"

"I want to say yes, but I'm constantly analyzing our relationship in my head."

"Stop analyzing and go with your heart." Victoria said.

"I'll tell you girls tomorrow after I give him my answer."

The next morning Kelsey packed her suitcase into the trunk and waited for the other girls by her car. Brody looked out the window of the guest house and saw her standing there alone. The other guys were still asleep. He crept out the door, being careful not to wake them.

"Thanks for coming to the party." He approached her.

"Thanks for inviting me. I'm sure we'll always remember the fun." Kelsey didn't want to make Brody any more nervous. "My answer is yes just in case you were wondering." She smiled.

He peered down at her lips and they slowly came together.

Beth and Victoria stood at the front door and happily screamed.

Brody and Kelsey looked over at them and laughed.

Chapter 13

A few months had passed in an instant.

"Mom, can you pass the egg rolls?" Kelsey sat at the dinner table with her parents and little brother later that day. She wished she had someone to talk to about the genetic testing of their family. If her parents found out, they would put an end to her investigation, and if she told her brother, he'd certainly squeal to her parents.

There was a knock on their door. "I'll get it." Her father pushed his seat back and went to answer it.

"Kelsey, its Miss Hall for you." He called from the front of the house.

She squashed up her face in a confused expression and walked to the door.

"Hi Kelsey, I need to borrow you for a moment. The Princess wanted me to ask you to visit the Dome Gardens at seven o'clock tonight. She has to gather information for her ladies garden club she just joined. I guess she is trying to have more in common with the Earl of Atherton."

"Okay, what does she need me to do?" Kelsey asked.

"Take notes and pictures of some flowers in the tropical biome."Abie informed.

"That's it?"

"Yes. I've included driving directions in case you haven't been there before." Miss Hall handed her a piece of paper.

"Actually I have several times when I was little."

"Great. She said you can call the palace tomorrow morning before you come over to show her."

"I get a meeting with her?" Kelsey beamed. She hadn't seen Victoria since Brody's birthday weekend.

"Yes, and at her specific request."

Kelsey couldn't believe it. Brody was helping to bring the family closer.

Later that night she pulled into the Dome Gardens. No one else was around. She got out of her car and entered the crisp, night air. The interior lights illuminated the tops of the four round shaped green houses. The fifth one appeared rather dim in comparison to the others. She walked closer to read the signs determining which one she needed to visit. The arrow pointed to the dimly lit dome.

"How are the pictures going to turn out if the lighting is poor? I'll have to find a switch." She pondered out loud and opened the door to the foyer. From the adjoining room, she could see the tall, swanky trees up lit in green, towering a protective leafy cover for the tropical flowers below. The water fall into the man-made pond, trickled gently, bouncing off the flag stone.

She walked into the dome and saw several, soft white candles edging the islands of huge, exotic flowers. The smell made her feel like she was in a privet oasis, far away from home.

All of her concerns dissipated. She detected light, smooth jazz music playing on the speakers hung in the air. She stepped into the middle of the dome and looked up through the large trees, revealing the clear, starry celestials.

"What a heavenly place." She gave a breathless sigh.

"I think so."

She turned around and saw Brody standing in the glow of it all at the entrance. He wore jeans and a black tee shirt.

"How? Why?" She shrugged her shoulders unable to speak.

He stepped closer to her and placed his finger on her lips. He put her hand on his shoulder and the other in his palm, and they swayed to the gentle rhythm of the music. This time she didn't fight it. What was the point? She wanted to enjoy the extreme elation she was feeling – an inner peace she had never known. She looked into his dreamy eyes and saw her reflection. His heart beat steady against her.

When the song ended, he let go of her and held up one finger. She clasped her hands together wondering what he was doing but felt comfortable about it. He came around the corner with a dark green, fleece blanket and picnic basket. "I figured we could have dessert under the sky tonight." He spoke softly not wanting to scare her away this time.

They sat on the blanket and he pulled out berries covered in chocolate, tiramisu and amaretto cheese cake. The myriad of decedent scents, released her apprehensions. There was no 'what ifs' tonight. It was simply her and Brody.

"Pick one." He suggested. "Or we could sample one of each?"

"I'll take the former idea." Her smile was genuine, not the fake one she was used to parading.

He pulled out a fork and fed her a bite. She reveled in the creamy flavors, sending her taste buds soaring over the full moon like a comet.

When dessert had ended, he leaned back on one arm looking upward and patted the blanket for her to relax next to him. She wiggled to find a comfy spot where she fit into his arms.

"I must confess, the Princess and I have been planning this night for quite some time."

"She was in on this?"

"It took work and lots of patience to break through your barriers, but so worth it." He stared into her eyes.

She grabbed the back of his neck and pulled him closer. Their sugar coated lips touched in a slow deliberate love. He put his arms around her as they remained locked together.

It was the perfect kiss – trusting, passionate, and lovingly selfless. She wanted to give him the world and he wanted to give her the heavens.

"Close your eyes." He commanded.

She did as he asked. She heard a rustling in front of her.

"Alright, open them."

She gasped.

He was on one knee with a diamond ring between his out stretched fingers.

"We have known each other for five months, but I'm letting God guide my heart. I want to have you in my life everyday." A tear slid down his cheek. "Please be my wife?" His hands were trembling with hope.

"Yes." She grinned back, wiped the tear from his blushed face and kissed him tenderly.

"I hope this fits, because I never want you to take it off." He laughed placing the ring on her finger. "I want everyone to know you're mine!"

"I want nothing more than that either." She hugged him.

Chapter 14

Three months passed quickly with planning the wedding. She had selected Beth and Princess Victoria as her bridesmaids. Brody chose her little brother and his older one as groomsmen.

"I can't believe that next year you'll be a married woman." Beth thought with a stack of travel magazines in front of her. She was helping Kelsey pick a location for their honeymoon.

"I'm sure you want to tell me 'I told you so'." Kelsey laughed.

"How about, I knew it."

"Perfect." They both chuckled.

The doorbell chimed.

"I'm not expecting anyone." Beth got up to go open it. "Hi Uncle Clark."

Kelsey dropped her brochure and ran to the entrance.

"Hi girls, I came by to ask if you want me to apply for the exhumations or not."

"Come in and have a seat." Beth led them back to the living room.

He sat down on an oversized chair. "Kelsey, it is important for you to remember that this could either go positively or negatively, but understand that if you do decide to do this, I will protect the respectability of your deceased loved ones and your present family."

"I know you will." Kelsey sighed. *Over three hundred years of history is resting on my shoulders! God, why does it have to be up to me to make this decision?"*

She had gone over the consequences in her mind a million times. She kept coming back to the idea that if she is doing it all for the right reasons, then the outcome will be good as well. Now that it had come down to the final decision, Kelsey was second guessing her original choice.

Beth sensed a struggle going on in Kelsey's mind. Then, she had an idea of how to help her friend. "Who is the One that knows everything?"

She looked at Beth blankly not catching on.

"Here is another clue. Who is the One who walks before us and if we ask, will help guide us in the right direction?"

"The Lord." Kelsey replied.

"What do you think the Lord wants out of all this?"

"I think He has a plan for each one of us to grow closer to Him."

"Do you think your family will continue to go along the same paths as they have been, if things are not shaken up a little?"

"You mean, suppressing the truth?" Kelsey asked.

Beth nodded.

"What do you think?" Kelsey turned toward Uncle Clark.

"You can't get more direct than God. Also, know that it is me who is willing to answer questions from the media. I will be delivering the results of the DNA tests."

"Should I search the law of parliament first before letting this happen? I never anticipated we would be able to prove the secrets." Kelsey asked.

"That is up to you, but I'll need an answer by the end of the week," Clark said.

Kelsey glanced at Beth with a raised brow.

"Yes, we can go check it out if it will make you feel better." Beth replied.

She clapped her hands several times with a smile on her freckled face.

Chapter 15

The next morning, Kelsey and Beth found themselves sitting on an old, stone fence six hundred yards from the exhumation site at the graveyard.

"I'm going to need another cup of coffee to get me going this early." Beth declared.

"I wish there was another way around this." Kelsey stated.

"We went over it several times. This is the only way to be sure of who is who. Once we know the results of the DNA tests we can start putting the pieces together." Beth said.

Kelsey stared at the morning fog blurring the Environmental Health Officer, Uncle Clark, and the religious authorities. "How long do you think this will take?"

"Not sure, but it looks like they are finally loading something into the van. We should go meet them at the lab." Beth jumped off the fence and waved her arm for Kelsey to follow her to the car.

They arrived at the lab and waited ten minutes for the van to pull up in a space next to them. The girls quickly got out of the vehicle and ran over to Uncle Clark.

He started to open the back doors and grabbed white, plastic totes. They followed him into the building to the guard station. He showed his badge. "These girls are assisting me today."

The guard nodded and let them all pass. They entered a door where he slid his badge across a scanner. It opened slowly and they walked along a sterile, white painted hallway with white tiles toward a double door entrance.

The anticipation mixed with having not eaten breakfast, made Kelsey dizzy. Her eyes only detected black and white and then she dropped.

She awoke on a twin bed in a small, blue room. Her vision was fuzzy at first and then Brody's face came into a clear image.

"What are you doing here?" Kelsey inquired.

"Beth called me when you fainted. I came as soon as I could." He stroked her hand.

"Where am I?"

"You're still at the lab. This is the nurse's station where they take blood and stuff," he replied.

"Brody, do you know what's going on?" Kelsey asked.

"No. Beth said you would explain it to me when you felt better. But first my main concern is you." He handed her orange juice and an oatmeal cookie. "I thought this might perk you up a bit. Eat this and when you finish you can tell me everything."

She did as told. "Where is Beth?" She chewed on her last bite of cookie.

"She is with her uncle." He said.

"How long was I out? Did I miss anything? Do they have the results?" Kelsey's anticipation grew.

"I've got no information here. They said you would get me up to date. So what is this all about?" Brody questioned.

"Well, I probably should have told you earlier." She sat up. Her head throbbed on the back. She closed her eyes for a moment. "Do you think you could search for some pain medicine first?"

He rummaged through the cabinets and found a bottle of them and filled a small paper cup full of water. She took the pills and began telling the story.

He sat in stunned silence attempting to figure out the questions he had.

Beth opened the blue door. "Kels, you're awake! The nurse told me you'd be alright so I went to run the test with my uncle. I was just coming to check on you. How do you feel?"

"I've got a little headache, but you might want to direct your question to Brody."

"You told him?" Beth's jaw dropped.

"Yep." Kelsey replied.

"So what do you think of all this?" Beth inquired.

"It's strange. Somehow I never thought I'd live through a monumental period of history as this will turn out to be." Brody said.

"We obviously don't know what to make of it either." Kelsey admitted.

"The test should be completed soon." Beth stared at her watch. "Since I know you are now in good hands, I'm going to go check on things."

Kelsey started to throw her legs over the edge of the bed.

"Oh, no you don't." Brody warned.

She rolled her eyes and got comfortable again.

Fifteen minutes went by before Beth came back with her uncle.

"What's the news?" Kelsey inquired.

They joined Brody on the couch nearest the wall.

"I first want to know how we're going to handle the press outside." Brody asked thinking for Kelsey.

"Very carefully, we will say 'no comment' until we inform Kelsey's family."

"So what is the verdict?" Kelsey questioned.

"We found that the mtDNA, which is the maternal line of Azuriah matched with Flora's. The Y line DNA test from Duke Dane resulted in a close match with Flora's as well."

"What about Graham?" Kelsey searched his face for answers.

"His did not match Azuriah's or resemble Duke Dane's, which basically proves he is adopted."

"So, Graham is our ancestor who got to live the life of a Prince. Flora's lineage consists of actual royals who don't even know it?" Kelsey interpreted.

"Yes." Uncle Clark said.

"What about the marriage the Duke had? If Flora was his and Azuriah's child, then why didn't *they* marry?" Kelsey asked.

"Who says they didn't?" The Uncle fed them information. "Duke Dane had a feeling all this would surface someday, so he had his friend, Lord Wyn Northrop, place a letter on his chest in his casket. Once we found that, all the questions were answered." He looked around the room at all of them.

"So, you didn't *have* to run a DNA test?" Kelsey asked.

"We did run the tests just to verify. We didn't want to get to this point and have arguable evidence," Clark pointed out.

"What did the note say?" Brody asked.

"I'll let you read the whole letter in a few days. The lab team is preserving it right now." He sighed. "The Duke and Azuriah secretly married and that is when she became pregnant with Flora."

"Then why didn't they stay together?" Kelsey wondered.

"Here is how lies can build up. One of the Duke's friends named Trestan Stowe, was actually his enemy and threatened the couple because she was a commoner. Trestan was hoping the Duke wouldn't have any heirs and he would become Duke Dane's successor."

"I've seen a painting of Trestan and the Duke hanging in the Palace! It identifies him as his best friend." Kelsey remembered.

"The King, not knowing they were married or with child sent Azuriah away from the Duke. Rupert, in return, agreed to let her go, after Trestan threatened to harm them. He was going to send for her, but the King was dying and wanted to pass his title on to him right away." Uncle Clark stroked his mustache. "The King called for him and in his refusal to marry another, decided to forge a marriage without Trestan knowing any of this. Ten months passed and with the help of his friend, Wyn Northrop, the Duke adopted a newborn boy. He had been orphaned by war and was given the name Graham."

"What happened to Flora and Azuriah?" Brody wanted answers.

"During that same time, Flora was born. He wrote the same birth date on Graham's certificate in an attempt to pay honor to Flora and to join them as sister and brother." Clark explained.

"So, why didn't they become a family?" Kelsey piped in.

"The news of the marriage and birth went public. That sealed his fate with Azuriah forever." The creases around Clark's mouth echoed his frown. "She died of a broken heart a few days later after hearing that he had married and had a child, not knowing it was a fake marriage."

"Remember they said the fake Duchess died while giving birth? At that time, she could have come back to him without the public knowing anything wrong had happened if she had only known the truth." Beth remarked.

"Precisely." Her Uncle added.

"We have to find Flora's side of the family and tell them!" Kelsey added.

"Hold your horses." Brody stood up. "You have got to think of the consequences first."

"Yes, but the reporters are already outside waiting to hear." Kelsey could not escape the confusion.

Clark reclined in his chair. "We don't have to reply until we can figure the best way to handle it."

"Her Majesty should be informed first, out of respect. Don't you think?" Beth handed Kelsey a glass of water.

She drank a few sips. "I'll call Abie Hall and ask her to schedule me an appointment to speak with the Queen. I want to do a little research to find Flora's bloodline, just so I have it to show her."

Chapter 16

Brody paced in the small study at Kelsey's parent's home.

She was rapidly typing searches at various genealogical websites.

"You have been at this for hours!" Brody said.

"I'm on a roll." Her fingers clicked on the keyboard. "Here we go." She pressed the enter button.

Brody leaned over her shoulder. The computer screen zipped from page to page, displaying vertical lines and names in a blur.

Kelsey squinted and bobbed her head right and left.

"It is going too fast to read it. Wait until it prints out." Brody suggested.

"How much paper do you think we'll need?" Kelsey asked.

His eyes grew bigger and he stared at her.

She placed the stack of paper into the machine and hit the print button.

Once it was finished, she grabbed her high lighter and followed the lines to the last family on record.

"Now what are you doing?" Brody asked.

"Checking the online phone book." Kelsey said.

"You're not going to pick up the phone and call them are you?"

"No. It should give an address along with their number."

"Are you going to march right up to their door step and say, 'hey, guess what? It's you're lucky day?'" Brody's voice grew with intensity.

"Come with me?" She pleaded.

"I know you called Abie to set up a meeting, did she reply?" He asked.

"No, she didn't call me back."

"Kels, it has been two weeks already."

"I know. My intuition told me not to trust Abie, so I also sent a letter directly to Her Majesty." Kelsey said.

"And?"

"I'm seeing her this afternoon. That is why I was so pressed to find this family tree. What's interesting, is even though I'm not biologically related to Duke Dane and Azuriah, I feel a connection with this other family."

The screen popped up revealing the information.

Kelsey pointed to the computer. "Brody, get me a pen and paper." Her eyes began to well up.

He handed her the pen and saw the anguish in the reflection of her tears. "What's wrong?" He kneeled down beside her chair.

"I don't know. It is all so strange. Will this family accept me or see me as a threat once they find out what they may be entitled to?"

"No one can predict that." Brody placed the palms of his hands on her checks. "You just have to hope for the best. If the best doesn't happen, well, you've done your part by setting the truth free."

"It's not like we're related, so they don't have to be a part of my life. Is it weird to want them to be?" Kelsey anguished.

"No. Try not to pre-label them so you won't be disappointed."

She took the writing utensil from his hand and wrote with a deep breath. "Their names are Gideon and Kayla Meriwether."

"It says here they live out on Meadow Brook Road." Brody added.

"Do you know where that is?" Kelsey asked.

"I've traveled the countryside extensively while I was studying right before school let out. It is in the middle of farm land I believe." Brody said.

"Will you come with me to see the Queen?"

"I think this is a family affair. I want the two of you to be comfortable talking without her wondering whether Her Majesty can trust me or not. She might be a little upset with me for not falling for her daughter."

"I see your point." Kelsey got up and walked over to get her purse and keys. "Pray things will go smoothly and that God's purpose will be accomplished."

"Of course." He waved from the driveway before getting into his yellow jeep.

Chapter 17

Kelsey was escorted to the main office in the palace. Abie Hall was sitting at her desk on the phone. She nodded at the guard to leave and motioned for her to sit down.

"May I help you?" Able asked after hanging up.

"Her Majesty is expecting me."

"Really?" She rifled through the Post-Its on her calendar desk. "I was not informed of this. You know you may not get in to see her if you do not have a scheduled time."

"Listen Abie, I…"

"It is Miss Hall."

Fine, you want to play that game? Kelsey fumed. "Why don't you call her?"

"Being her Personal Assistant, I happen to know she has another engagement right now."

"Why are you doing this?" Kelsey asked.

"Doing what?" Abie played dumb.

Kelsey leaned on her desk with both arms and lowered her face half a foot from Abie's.

"I have patiently put up with your rude behavior for some time now and things are going to be done the right way from now on. Is that understood Miss Hall?"

Abie reached under the desk and hit the rewind button on the video player of the surveillance camera. "You don't scare me. Go ahead and see for yourself." Abie slowly waved her arm toward the T.V.'s screen display of the Queen's meeting room.

She was with several Lords from Parliament seated at an oval table.

"You win. I'll be leaving now." Kelsey strolled back to the foyer and waited a few minutes. She tiptoed, returning to the office door and peered around the corner.

Abie's back was facing her. She held a remote up to the camera and was resetting it to real time.

Kelsey turned with her back against the open door. *I've got to remember where the meeting room is!* She had been there a year before on a tour of the palace.

Guards were positioned at every entrance and exit. No one was paying attention to her. She headed around the corner where it was vacant and toward the fire alarm. She broke the little window and pulled the handle. A shrill siren pierced the air.

The guard at the elevator evacuated his stance and ran toward the sound. She scurried to the lift and tapped the 'up' button several times and looked behind her. The doors opened and she bolted in. Kelsey pressed the 'close doors' and saw a guard rushing to her. The doors blocked him just in time.

She knew she wouldn't have long before they would try to stop the elevator, so she got off on the next floor, below where she needed to be. She raced to the open stair well and dashed up the slippery, marble stairs. The tread of her shoe slipped out from under her and her shin hit on the edge of a step. She sat crippled in throbs of pain. *Only four more steps!*

Kelsey looked upward. She hopped to one foot and pulled herself along the railing. She lay down on the cold tile floor and crawled to the room. A guard quickly intervened before she could get to the door way.

The Queen heard the struggle and a recognizable voice in the hall and decided to see what was going on. She saw the man trying to pull Kelsey to her feet.

Tears flowed down her porcelain face.

"Let go of her." The Queen ordered and rushed to her side. "What in Heaven's name is going on?"

The elevator doors opened and Miss Hall stepped out. "Your Majesty! I didn't let her up to see you because she was threatening the staff."

"That is not true and you know it!" Kelsey sat on the floor.

"Miss Hall! You knew I had a meeting with my Great Niece today. Go back to your office. I will deal with you later."

"Yes, Your Highness." She reproached.

Her Majesty turned to Kelsey. "Let me help you up my dear. I must apologize for this wild behavior on my Assistant's part." She led her into the room and sat her on a comfortable chair. She bent down to take a look at the swelling on her leg. "That is going to be quite a goose egg. I will send for some ice to reduce the bruising." She handed her an embroidered hanky.

"Thank you."

"I will only admit this to you. Sometimes I wish my life was different." The Queen sighed.

"Do you miss Great Uncle Halton?" Kelsey asked.

"More than you know." She trailed off in thought.

The palace nurse interrupted. She investigated the sore and placed the ice on Kelsey's leg. "This should help. I will get you some pain medicine and take another look at it once you are done conversing."

"I had sent Miss Hall to keep you from finding out our family secrets Kelsey, but you must understand," she placed her hand on Kelsey's forearm, "there was no intention on my part of anyone getting hurt."

"Have you seen how centuries of covering the truth has led to a distance in the members of our family?" Kelsey asked.

"It has its disadvantages, but so does everything."

"Have you been watching the news?" Kelsey wondered.

"I was informed about the unanswered questions from the media at the lab."

"I know what happened all those years ago." Kelsey admitted.

"What do you know?" The Queen did not want to give out any more information than she had to.

Kelsey told of her adventures ending with the letter buried with Duke Dane and the DNA results.

"One thing is for sure, you are quite intelligent. Now we have to figure out how to keep this under wraps."

"What? No. I found Flora's bloodline." Kelsey stood up ignoring the pain in her leg. "They have to be told. They are the other half." She began to pace the floor. "In the Duke's letter, it said he wanted to bind Graham and Flora together as sister and brother. He attempted to do the right thing. We need to bring the two families together."

"Child, do you realize what would happen?" Her Majesty stood up and walked around the room. "Our country's laws in parliament declare the ruler is of the bloodline. Have you thought what that would mean for us?" She paused. "We are familiar with all facets of the law. Could you imagine strangers taking over? They would not know how to handle fame, wealth and power. It could destroy our country."

"Considering this unique situation, couldn't parliament amend the law?" Kelsey reflected.

"I do not even want to find out if they would do that or not!" The Queen replied.

"I have to think this information would require emergency meetings on their part." Kelsey said.

"It is all too risky. I have sacrificed so much to keep this a secret." Her Majesty looked upward.

"I have an idea. What if I meet the family first before they are told?" Kelsey asked.

"Yet again - too risky."

"I could drive the car around and conveniently run out of gas. I'll have Brody with me."

"What is prompting you to do this? Why won't you let this go?" The Queen shook her head.

"The truth needs to be told. It will unleash the chains you and our family are bound to."

"I have a duty to uphold." The Queen declared.

"If you do anything, will you ask for God's guidance in this matter? Promise me you'll pray about it." Kelsey requested.

"That I can and will do. Until then, nothing is spoken of this to anyone." Her Majesty finished.

Kelsey nodded.

The Queen retreated to the chapel of the palace. She was alone. The silence calmed her nerves. Her Majesty made the sign of the cross before entering the pew and pulled the kneeler down. She rested against the back of the bench in front of her and gathered her thoughts together in the presence of the Lord.

Christ, I pay honor to you for guiding me in matters of the country and heart. I need you more than ever and will rejoice on the day you return. You are my strength, my kindness and my grace to continue serving as the Queen.

I need your help to choose the proper thing to do. I can continue with silence, or speak out to reveal the truth. I do not want people to hurt from my decision, but if you show me the way, I will obey you and be at peace knowing it is the right choice for everyone involved. Please send me a sign. Amen.

Marabel arose from her position with determination. She must find Abie.

Miss Hall sat stiffly in her office chair. She smoothed out her suit, gaining her composer from the recent hustle.

Her Majesty entered the room. The wrinkles on her face leaned into a scowl.

Abie straightened the papers on her desk.

"Miss Hall? I need a word with you."

"Yes, Your Highness."

"Gather your belongings and get out from behind the desk. You no longer work here."

"But Your Majesty, I helped you keep this secret. Without me, Kelsey would have exposed everything."

"The way you handle people is the reason you are leaving. Your coldness and lack of emotion make me question your motives. I overheard you talking to a subordinate that you were getting in my 'good graces' and would be climbing the royal ladder."

Abie could not dispel what was already known. "I'll pack my things."

Chapter 18

"I spoke with parliament and they have agreed to consider an addendum. I would like to go ahead with your plans to contact Flora Dane's family." The Queen held the phone to her ear.

Kelsey placed her hand on her mouth. "I can't believe it. It is all coming together."

"I must admit I feel a huge weight lifted off of me." The Queen paused. "I'm not sure how the throne will be shared, but it might even help the country to utilize the knowledge of these people since they have lived as commoners for so long."

Beth, Brody and Kelsey piled into his jeep.

"Do you think they will recognize you or Brody from pictures or television?" Beth clicked her seat belt into its buckle.

"We are not in the news very often so I doubt it," Kelsey reflected.

They drove about an hour through the lush vineyards and orchards of the country side and parked off a dirt road amongst the tall grass. Hidden crickets chirped loudly and the cicadas' voices crescendoed and fell again.

"Here goes nothing." Kelsey straightened her posture and pulled at her blazer.

They strode up to the end of the long, dusty driveway. A small, white farm house emerged from the back of a hill.

A bright green, tractor was parked on the side of a smaller building and a red pick-up truck sat in the sun.

"I -I don't know if I can do this." Kelsey stammered.

"Of course you can. We are all in it together." Beth wrapped her arm around her friends.

"What if they don't like me?" Kelsey asked.

"I know I'm biased, but what's not to like?" Brody said.

Kelsey knocked on the strong, wooden door. "They're out back." She heard the faint voice of a woman.

She knocked harder.

"Comin'!" She yelled. The footsteps got louder. A petite, middle aged woman with black hair opened the door. She wiped her hands on her gingham red apron and looked them up and down.

"Hi, I'm Kelsey and these are my friends. We seem to be out of gas. Could we barrow some?"

"Oh sure, my husband is in the barn." She pointed to the white, three story building.

"What a gorgeous farm. What do you raise?" Brody complimented her.

"We have about three hundred cattle and lots of chickens. What are you guys doing way out here? You look dressed for the city."

"I'm studying botany at the university. There is so much to learn out in the country." Brody spoke up.

The woman's wrinkles deepened as she smiled. "I'm Kayla Meriwether." She shook their hands. They all introduced themselves.

They arrived at the tall wooden gate of the barn yard. A man in blue jean overalls was pitching hay into the cow stalls. He stopped and wiped the sweat from his tanned face when he saw them approaching. "This here is my husband Gideon. These kids are in need of some gas, honey."

"Alright, why don't you all get into the coolness of the house while I fetch it?"

"Would you enjoy some lemonade?" Kayla offered.

They gathered around a long table in the kitchen. Kelsey ran her fingers over the deep grooved scratches on its surface.

"Kids come down!" Kayla yelled up the stairs. A loud boom and crash resounded from the small downstairs. A stampede of children bolted into the room.

"This is Giana and Bailey, my nine and five year olds." She pointed at the girls matching blue jean dresses. "I made them myself."

"Very haute couture." Beth complimented her creativity.

"Now I don't speak any different languages," Kayla replied.

"It is a term used to describe clothes made specifically for one person from a house of design," Beth explained.

Kayla nodded and blushed. "Vincent and Sterling are behind the little ones."

Kelsey guessed they were preteens.

Vincent came forward to shake their hands. He had bleached blonde hair and freckles everywhere. Sterling remained shy and kept looking at the floor. She had red hair wrapped in tight, shoulder length curls.

"My oldest are Adam and Acacia. They are out somewhere in the pasture." She pulled up a chair. "Adam wants to take over the farm. Gideon is teaching him the business end of it. Acacia is enchanted by princesses and princes. I thought she might grow out of it, but she's been keeping up with all the gossip. I try to tell her it's probably all hogwash, but she believes it."

"What's in the tabloids these days?" Kelsey nervously bounced her knee.

"I guess a small band of people dug up the late King Rupert Dane and took him for tests at the lab. Why they would've done a thing like that is beyond me, but you can't trust everything you read."

Kelsey carefully sipped her icy, cold drink.

The screen door opened. Acacia's emerald green eyes popped against the pigment of her autumn leaf colored hair.

It hung long and straight against the small features of her face. She halted abruptly seeing the crowded room. Then her eyes fell on Kelsey.

She could tell she was recognized immediately.

Acacia then turned her gaze to Brody and gawked with an open mouth.

Her mother introduced her to everyone and mentioned her father was getting them gas.

"Well, you all could stay for dinner." Acacia spoke softly in an effort to hide her exhilaration.

Kayla glanced at her daughter acting out of character.

"Mom, can they stay?" Acacia prodded.

Kelsey sensed the mother's hesitation wondering if they didn't have enough food since their visit was unplanned. "That is kind of you to think of us, but we do have to get back soon. Perhaps I should give you my phone number and we could have you guys over sometime to thank you for helping us?"

A wide smile grew on Acacia's face. Her eyes lit up at the thought.

Chapter 19

Abie Hall strutted into the headquarters of the Gallant Tabloid and toward the receptionist's desk with a gleam in her eye.

"Gallant Tabs, can you hold?" The secretary switched between several calls and jotted messages in between. She saw the woman waiting before her and lifted one finger.

Abie smiled happily that she was not in this woman's shoes anymore.

She hung up the line and gave out a large breath. "How may I help you?"

"I am here to see a journalist," Abie hissed.

"Which one Miss?"

"Any of them."

"Do you have an appointment?"

Abie glared at her. "If you knew the information I had, you would get me one right away."

She lifted the phone to call an extension. "May I ask what it is pertaining to?"

"You can read it tomorrow." Her cold words froze any warmth that may have been in her body.

Abie marched into the writer's small office.

"If you are one of their best, then why is your office so diminutive?"

"I don't usually spend much time here because I'm busy gathering stories." His large frame towered over hers. "Don't waste my time. Cut to the chase."

"First, let's discuss the monetary reward for my information."

"Before I can give you a dollar amount, you need to at least tell me a general idea of what it is about."

"An exposed Royal Family secret hidden for centuries." She waved her hand through the air. "Do you understand now?"

He urgently grabbed the phone to dial his boss. He replayed her idea to him and received an offer amount. He turned back to Abie. "How is $30,000?"

She leaned into his face; their noses millimeters from touching. "Let me reiterate to you – a centuries old secret that will change history."

He wiped the sweat starting to form on his heavy brows. "$50,000?"

"Just fine, thank you. I'll take monthly payments please. When will this be printed?"

"I can have this replace some other junk and make it possible for next week's distribution. Alright, spill it." He pressed the button on his tape recorder.

"Happily." She offered all the knowledge she had up to the present with the exception of the new bloodline which was unbeknown to her. "The Queen has known about this but had been hiding it from us all!" She added.

Chapter 20

The Queen paced in her quarters then rang for her Publicity Coordinator, Shawn Scott.

"Mr. Scott, I'm sad to inform you that Miss Hall no longer works here. I have this feeling she might retaliate and I need you to be aware." She proceeded to tell him the secrets. "I need you to contact Kelsey Dane and request she come to the palace to discuss how we are going to inform Flora's descendants.

Kelsey's phone rang as they were all walking back to the car with Gideon. She stepped off to the side of the road and listened intently to Mr. Scott.

"Don't mention anything yet. The Queen wants to be with you when you tell them." Shawn replied.

"Let Her Majesty know that I will be there in an hour or two." Kelsey hung up.

They convened later that day to get their stories straight and to decide how to break it to the Meriwethers. Kelsey educated the Queen of the Meriwether family profile and smiled when she spoke about the children. "The mother, Kayla, is such a warm spirited woman. There may be a problem though. I noticed when Acacia looked at me, she knew who I was. I am hopeful that it won't leak to the press that we were there."

"Do you really think she would not tell her friends that she met Kelsey Dane and the Earl of Atherton?" The Queen asked.

"I can't be certain of that, but even if she did, would they believe her? Plus they are so far out in the country that it might take awhile for the information to leak to several people."

"We'll go tomorrow. We must. I do not want them hearing about their legacy from anyone other than myself." The Queen replied.

The following day Kelsey and the Queen packed a large picnic basket for them and the Meriwethers to share for lunch.

Her Majesty slipped on her white, wrist length gloves. "Do you have the DNA results?"

"Yes, Clark faxed them over last night. I've also got a copy of the family tree line traced back to Azuriah and Duke Dane from Kayla's Heritage," Kelsey responded.

"Then we're off." The Queen tapped on the window separating the front of the Rolls Royce from the back.

They pulled up to the dirt driveway. Her Majesty hesitated before walking toward their door. They both looked at each other with apprehension.

Acacia came to answer and recognized them both right away. "Oh my, Mamma, the Queen is here! See, I told you it was Kelsey Dane who came the other day!"

Kayla rushed to the front not believing her eyes. "Offer them to come in!" She led them to the couch. "It's not much, but we love it here."

"On behalf of the royal family…" the Queen politely cleared her throat, "On behalf of the royal *families,* I want to thank you for helping a stranger in need the other day."

"No problem." Kayla patted Acacia's leg who was sitting next to her. "We are honored to help anyone who needs it."

"There is something we must tell you." Her Majesty cleared her throat. "We want to let you know before you read it in the newspaper and such."

"Did a reporter follow Kelsey and her friends out here? You need us to sign a release for a picture they took, don't you?" Kayla figured.

"No. What you are about to hear, will change your life. I hope for the better, but I'm sure that each person will react in their own way. Some might think it for the worse."

"I can assure you, Your Highness, we make every attempt at looking for the positive in situations." Kayla said.

The Queen revealed most of the story.

Kelsey interjected with how she came into the picture by finding Azuriah's earring, the love letters, fake documents and the sister and brother's gravestones."

"What a tale!" Kayla fiddled with the cross on her necklace. "There is another family, then?"

Kelsey took the papers out of her purse and gave them to Kayla. Acacia peered over her slender shoulder at the clearly defined lines.

"This can't be." Kayla shook her head.

"Tell me about what you know of your family history?" Kelsey attempted to help her put the pieces together.

"I mean, I've always heard silly rumors of the time when my Great, Great, Great Grandma met a Duke, but I just figured it was a beautiful fairy tale."

"It is your *family* tale." Kelsey said.

"No. If that story were true and if we are who you say we are, then we would've grown up with you." Kayla didn't understand.

The Queen finished the story.

"We were separated by lies the devil used to break our family apart?" Acacia asked.

"Basically." Kelsey replied.

They all sat in a stunned silence.

"Well, I guess those reporters will be all over our farm soon."

"A lot more than that will change for you." Kelsey broke the ice. "My Great Aunt, already told Parliament and they are working on an addendum to change the law. She requested that both families be involved in ruling the country."

The blood drained out of Kayla's face.

"You mean we're moving to the palace?" Acacia jumped out of her seat.

The Queen finished chewing her bite of salad. "I'm not sure how this is going to play out. Parliament has yet to come to a conclusion. We wanted you to know before the general public so you would have fair warning and discuss with your family how you will deal with that part of it."

Acacia hugged Kelsey. "Can we be like sisters?"

She thought for a second. "Yeah, I'd like that. Just because we are not directly related by blood, doesn't mean we are not related by God."

After the shock had worn off, they took the picnic outside by a small pond on their property. Gideon and the rest of the children saw them beyond the pasture and joined in.

Her Majesty patted her mouth with a napkin. "I want to invite your side of the family to a royal reunion at the palace in a few weeks."

Yells and squeals escaped their lips.

Acacia looked down.

"What's wrong?" Kelsey asked.

"I don't have anything to wear."

"Not yet!" She giggled back. "Just wait until you see what I have picked out for you – only if you like it of course. There are many clothes to choose from."

"I can't believe this." Tears eagerly ran down her face. "It's my dream come true."

"It is for us too." Kelsey remarked.

Chapter 21

Kelsey, Princess Victoria, Brody and Beth gathered at the top of the terrace at the late Duke Dane's castle.

"This is the perfect location for our family reunion!" Kelsey could smell the fragrance of the roses blown from the gentle breeze the afternoon offered.

The gardeners had decorated the grounds with freshly planted hostas and wisteria along the arbors and pergolas. A large bronze statue was erected in celebration of the two families coming together. Waiters hustled about carrying silver platters of hors d'oeuvres.

Tables with various crafts were stationed in a corner for the children and croquet was set up to the side of it. The Queen had a chart of the family tree propped against a black easel.

"I have some one for you to meet." The Princess addressed her friends.

They all followed her onto the main garden and over to Shawn Scott. She put her arm in his. "This is our first public appearance together as boyfriend and girlfriend." She gushed.

"But how did this happen? I thought you weren't allowed to date because he worked for the Palace?" Kelssy asked.

"I know, but once I sat down with my mother and explained that I have loved him for quite some time, she couldn't resist being happy for us."

Shawn smiled at Victoria. "I had always admired her and we'd steal glances when we were in the same room, but I had no idea she liked me too." He kissed her on her forehead.

"I'm so happy for you guys." Kelsey responded.

"I hear congratulations are in order for your upcoming nuptials." Princess Victoria winked at Brody.

"The planning is coming right along. We have dress and tux fittings tomorrow." Brody put his arm around his soon-to-be bride.

"They're here!" Kelsey saw the Meriwethers appear at the French doors leading onto the main terrace. The girls wore exquisite, golden gowns made by the palace designer. They each fashioned a different cut. All of the guys had black tuxes with white, button down dress shirts.

"They look amazing." Beth stood in awe. "I never could have expected such a fabulous ending to our wild adventure."

"I know, and this is just the beginning." Kelsey replied.

All of the invited media pointed their camera at the two families. The Queen, Kelsey and the rest of their line, walked up to meet the royal bloodline. Each went for a hand shake, then the Meriwether clan pulled the Dane's in for a hug. Laughs and giggles were heard in the air. Camera flashes were going off everywhere.

"I think I'm blinded now." Beth remarked.

A small orchestra began to play upbeat jazz on a stone patio below.

Mrs. Short whispered into the Queen's ear.

Her Majesty walked over to the band and took the microphone into her hands. "Attention everyone, I have been told the Lords of Parliament have just arrived. They will announce their decision now as to how the country will be ruled."

A man approached the Queen and took the microphone. "I am Lord Grant. The new addendum to the law is completed. There will be a four year transition where the present ruling party will continue, and the Meriwethers will be integrated into the system to develop their knowledge of rules, regulations and general information." He paused. "At the completion of the four years, both parties will come together to form a whole." Lord Grant coughed. "Each person will have their place as their God given talents are acquired and or recognized. The law will be available to read in a few days. We wanted to announce the verdict to the royal families before the public is notified. Carry on with your celebration."

Shouts and cheers echoed, setting the mood for the remainder of the night.

Chapter 22

The year quickly passed.

"Acacia, this wedding will show you just how royal you are now." Beth snapped her gum. They carried their bridesmaid gowns in a thick plastic garment bag to Kelsey's convertible.

"Hurry up guys or we'll be late picking up Victoria." She shifted from park to drive with her foot on the brake.

They gently laid the dresses next to Kelsey's and jumped over the car door into their seats.

"How should I address the Princess?" Acacia asked.

"Now that we are family you can call her by her first name, but in public it is always by title." Kelsey informed.

"Trying to memorize all the rules and what to do in different situations is so complicated!" Acacia flustered.

They pulled up to the palace gates and waited for security to open them. They drove through the half circle and stopped at the main doors.

Victoria clenched her purse handles in her mouth, the dress hung off her arm and she held the cosmetic bag in her other hand. "Help." She muffled.

"Pop the trunk Kels." Beth grabbed some of the things. "Do you normally pack so…light?"

"Funny." Victoria quipped. "Kelsey, I remember when you were so bull headed thinking that Brody was for me. It took quite awhile to break you of that stubborn streak."

"You *think* that is what it was. Even I thought so until Brody made me realize I had to love myself before I could love anyone else. He was so true."

They rounded the bend toward the castle. "I can see it from here! Are you getting nervous?" Beth poked Kelsey in the side.

"Stop, I'm trying to keep us on the road! And for the record, I'm not nervous, just extremely excited to see his face from down the aisle."

The lot was full of expensive vehicles.

The girls ran into the castle giggling and found the guest room where they were all to get dressed.

"Look at this place!" Acacia's eyes spanned the 1600s décor. A large mahogany four poster bed was swaged in dark green velvet. The wooden floors creaked beneath her light movements.

Kelsey hung her wedding gown over top of the closet door. She slowly unzipped the garment bag savoring every moment of her day. "Beth, I want to thank you now for designing all the dresses. Once I put this on, I'm going to be a crying mess."

"It was the least I could do for you." Beth hugged her tightly. "It is just an added bonus that they will be pictured in all the major magazines." She laughed. "With my sketches and Kayla's sewing ability, we are able to pull this miracle together."

"I will have to thank her profusely." Kelsey said.

"Go on, I want to see what you think of it. Most brides see their dress before the wedding day, but I couldn't help surprising you." Beth said.

All the girls gathered around as Kelsey pulled it out of the bag. They gasped in awe of Beth's creation.

The heart shaped neck line dripped with pink, hand sewn crystals. It flowed off the shoulder and into a three fourth arm sleeve. The corset came to a 'v' at the waist where the petticoat was attached. The open middle of the rounded skirt mirrored the bodice with the pink accents.

"You're designing mine when I get married!" Victoria picked up a weighted piece of the material.

Beth held her rosy glow. "Most of it is pure silk." She lifted the skirt to reveal a hoop and cotton liner. "Didn't think you'd get away without one of these did you?"

Kelsey laughed. "I have no words." Then she began to cry.

"Don't tear up or your mascara will run. Let's get you into this." Victoria added.

"How?" Kelsey wondered.

Beth held her hand while she lifted one leg and then the other.

Victoria and Acacia pulled each side of the dress up and helped maneuver her arms in the sleeves. The gown scalloped into a long 'v' down her back.

Beth pulled the laces and tied them just above her bottom. "Turn around."

Kelsey admired herself in the long, oval swivel mirror. "I simply could not ask for anything more."

"I hope you would! You're missing the veil and tiara for goodness sake." Beth said.

Acacia ran back to the bag and pulled out the items. She stuck the comb attached to the eight foot long veil, just below her curl pinned bun sitting on top her head.

Beth placed the floral shaped tiara in front of the curls.

"I'll do my make up while you girls get ready." Kelsey began to nervously shake.

"You are still not done, sweetie." Beth brought her a shimmering silver cape with hood and slits for the arms and helped her put it on.

"Now, that is complete elegance." Acacia gushed.

"I feel on top of the world." Kelsey admitted.

"Good. That was the feeling I wanted you to get from this." Beth turned toward the others. "And for us, we have the matching pink bridesmaid gowns with black gloves that, yes ladies, go all the way up."

"Holy tamoly." Acacia reflected.

The girls stopped what they were doing.

"I'm still working on my *verbiage* in the royal classes." Acacia said.

Kelsey slipped into her glass heels and walked to the thin window looking over the back lawn toward the chapel.

The ladies exited the castle and stepped up into a white, horse drawn carriage lined in gray velvet. The driver made a noise, and the two black horses with matching gray tassels on their heads galloped away.

Brody placed one foot in front of the other going over the wedding rehearsal in his mind. He slowly approached the Minister at the front of the chapel and took his place. His gleaming eyes traced the arches of branches that connected the first and last pews. Garlands of greens and red roses hung from them. The middle pews supported spiral candelabras with pink glowing candles on its silver holders.

The stringed quartet played an introductory song as the bridesmaids and groomsmen took their walk down the silver path. Giana, Bailey and Sterling entered holding wicker, red hearts, stuffed with pink rose petals that floated to the ground every time they shook them.

Vincent realized he was too old to be a ring bearer, but didn't have the courage to tell Kelsey when she had asked him. He took his place near Brody, his older brother and Kelsey's little brother.

The heavy wooden doors opened, draping a strong ray of sunlight down the walk way.

Kelsey and her Dad stood side by side. She tapped his arm and nodded that it was time.

Brody stood in his black tux and pink tie with his hands held together. His hair was parted on the side and gelled in place. He whispered 'I love you' and the words floated to her lips. All she could think of was being able to love him forever.

After the exchange of vows and rings, Mr. and Mrs. Bronson got into the carriage and made their way to the reception at the castle's conservatory. Black table clothes adorned hundreds of round tables with pink, linen napkins shaped into swans. Eiffel Tower bud vases sat in the middle, with cascading pink and red roses.

At each place on the bridal party table laid tiny silver boxes. "There better not be something pink inside." Vincent commented.

Kelsey giggled. "Open them." She requested.

The girls found silver bracelets with a cross charm. "You can add more charms." Kelsey pointed out.

The guys held up their old fashioned pocket watches. "Turn them over," Brody said. "We engraved your initials on the back."

After a scrumptious dinner of seafood and pasta dishes, Beth made her way over to the desert table. Layers of strawberries encircled a chocolate fondue fountain. She dipped a few and watched Kelsey and Brody smash a too-gorgeous-to-eat wedding cake into each other's faces.

Victoria and her boyfriend Shawn stepped out onto the terrace for some air. The trees were decorated with white twinkle lights and a huge ice sculpture of a bride and groom kissing sat in pink lighting.

Shawn's love for the Princess had grown over the years. He enjoyed playing polo together and helping her deliver her poodle's puppies. He was hoping to be able to win over her heart that night. Many occasions had left him without the ability for words. Now, with few people mingling about, he gathered all his courage and pulled a soft, black box out of his tux coat pocket.

"This is something that symbolizes how much I feel for you." He knelt down on both knees and handed her the box.

At that moment, everyone turned and whispered.

Victoria's words caught in her throat and tears welled in her hazel eyes. She opened it to reveal an intricate pattern of diamonds in a platinum setting.

"That was your mother's and her mom's before." Shawn said.

"How did you get this?"

"I asked Her Majesty for her blessing and she gave it to me."

"Will you be mine forever?"

"Finally!" She teased him. "Do you know how long I've waited?"

He pulled her into a passionate embrace and twirled her around.

"Let's not tell Kelsey until they get back from their honeymoon." Victoria beamed. " I want this day to be about them."

Glossary

A

Addendum - textual matter that is added onto a publication; usually at the end
Adirondack - An icon of the Adirondacks, this classic chair harks back to the early days of the Great Camps in the Adirondacks.
Adjacent - nearest in space or position; immediately adjoining without intervening space; "had adjacent rooms"
Adrenaline - A catecholamine secreted by the adrenal medulla in response to stress. It stimulates autonomic nerve action.
Ambled - walk leisurely
Ancestors - someone from whom you are descended (but usually more remote than a grandparent)
Appendix – part of the intestines
Artifacts - a man-made object
Askew - turned or twisted toward one side

B

Bodice - part of a dress above the waist
Botany - the branch of biology that studies plants

C

Census - a period count of the population
Chaise - a long chair; for reclining
Charade - a composition that imitates somebody's style in a humorous way

Cloisonné - having areas separated by metal and filled with colored enamel and fired
Commoner - a person who holds no title
Conservatory - a greenhouse in which plants are arranged in a pleasing manner
Coquettish - talk or behave amorously, without serious intentions
Cordial - showing warm and heartfelt friendliness
Corset - a woman's close-fitting foundation garment
Croquet - a game in which players hit a wooden ball through a series of hoops; the winner is the first to traverse all the hoops and hit a peg.

D

Descendants - the offspring produced in any generation
Diminutive - very small
Dispel - force to go away
Divulge - make known to the public information that was previously known only to a few people or that was meant to be kept a secret
DNA - Deoxyribo**n**ucleic **a**cid is the primary chemical component of chromosomes and the material of which genes are made. It is sometimes called the "molecule of heredity," because parents transmit copied portions of their own DNA to offspring during reproduction and because in doing so they propagate their traits.
mtDNA - the DNA found in the many mitochondria found in each cell of a body. The sequencing of mitochondrial DNA can link individuals descended from a common female ancestor.

Y-line DNA - the Y chromosome in the nuclear DNA is being used to establish family ties. The Y chromosomal DNA test (usually referred to as Y DNA or Y-Line DNA) is only available for males, since the Y chromosome is only passed down the male line from father to son. Tiny chemical markers on the Y chromosome create a distinctive pattern, known as a haplotype that distinguishes one male lineage from another. Shared markers can indicate relatedness between two men, though not the exact degree of the relationship. Y chromosome testing is most often used by individuals with the same last name to learn if they share a common ancestor.
Dynasty - a succession of rulers who are members of the same family. The author uses this term to describe a succession of the character's friendship.

E

Earl - a British peer ranking below a Marquis and above a Viscount.
Elation - an exhilarating psychological state of pride and optimism
Entails - impose, involve, or imply as a necessary accompaniment or result
Evidence - your basis for belief or disbelief
Excavate - find by digging in the ground
Exhibit - to present or expose to view; show; display
Exhumed - (Exhumation) Dig up for reburial or for medical investigation; of dead bodies.
Exquisite - lavishly elegant and refined
Exuberant - joyously unrestrained

F

Facade - a showy misrepresentation intended to conceal something unpleasant
Faux - not genuine or real
Fiasco - an ambitious project that ends as a ridiculous failure
Foliage - leaves, as of a plant or tree; mass of leaves; leafage
Fondue - hot sauce-like melted cheese or chocolate in which bread or fruits are dipped

G

Genetics - the branch of biology that deals with heredity (genes) and variation in similar or related animals and plants

H

Haute Couture - trend-setting fashions
Heirs - a person who is entitled by law or by the terms of a will to inherit the estate of another
Hoisted - move from one place to another by lifting
Hors d'oeuvres - a food or foods intended to be eaten with the fingers

I

Illuminated - make lighter or brighter
Inevitable - incapable of being avoided or prevented
Infertile - incapable of reproducing
Insatiable - impossible to satiate or satisfy
Integrated - become one
Interlaid - to lay or place among or between
Intermittent - stopping and starting at irregular intervals

Intervened - get involved, usually so as to hinder or halt an action
Intrigue - cause to be interested or curious
Intuition - instinctive knowing (without the use of rational processes)

L

Leukemia - major type of cancer
Lineage - the descendants of one individual
Lords - used as a title for certain high officials and dignitary

M

Mahogany - wood of any of various mahogany trees; much used for cabinetwork and furniture
Medieval - characteristic of the time of chivalry and knighthood in the Middle Ages
Monumental - of outstanding significance

N

Nobility - a privileged class holding hereditary titles
Nonchalantly - a casual disregard

O

Obligation - a personal relation in which one is indebted for a service or favor
Oblique - slanting or inclined in direction
Ornate - rich in decorative detail

P

Paparazzi - a derogatory term for news photographers, especially those who invade the privacy of their subjects or who follow them relentlessly in search of a photo
Parliament - a legislative assembly in certain countries
Peerage - The titles within the peerage are, in ascending order of rank; baron (baroness for women), viscount (viscountess), earl (countess), marquess (marchioness), and duke (duchess).
Permeated - to pass into or through and affect every part of
Pergolas - a framework that supports climbing plants
Petticoat - undergarment worn under a skirt.
Postulated - a proposition that is accepted as true in order to provide a basis for logical reasoning
Princess Royale - the eldest daughter of a British sovereign, who has had the title conferred on her for life by the sovereign
Profusely - expressed at length, many times, and in many words
PH - is the measure of the acidity or alkalinity. The pH of soil or more precisely the pH of the soil solution is very important because soil solution carries in it nutrients such as Nitrogen (N), Potassium (K), and Phosphorus (P) that plants need in specific amounts to grow, thrive, and fight off diseases. Herbicides, pesticides, fungicides and other chemicals are used on and around plants to fight off plant diseases and get rid of bugs that feed on plants and kill plants. Knowing whether the soil pH is acidic or basic is important because if the soil is too acidic the applied pesticides, herbicides, and fungicides will not be absorbed (held in the soil) and they will end up in garden water and rain water runoff, where they eventually become pollutants in our streams, rivers, lakes, and ground water.

Publicist - a person who is an expert in or writes on current public or political affairs

R

Reciprocated - act, feel, or give in return
Reclusive - withdrawn from society; seeking solitude
Rectify - to put or set right; correct; amend
Regulations - is the control of something by rules
Rendition - a version or type of something
Renounce - give up, such as power, as of monarchs and emperors, or duties and obligations
Repercussions - an often indirect effect, influence, or result that is produced by an event or action
Reproached - an instance of charging oneself with a fault or mistake

S

Sanctuaries – a place where someone feels at peace
Sashayed - to walk with a lofty proud gait, often in an attempt to impress others
Seminar - any meeting for an exchange of ideas.
Sous-Chef - assumes responsibility for kitchen in absence of Head Chef

T

Tampered - fool or play around with
Teak - hard strong durable yellowish-brown wood of teak trees; resistant to insects and to warping; used for furniture and in shipbuilding

Terrace - a series of flat platforms of earth with sloping sides, rising one above the other, as on a hillside
Tiramisu - the Italian dessert made from lady fingers, espresso coffee, mascarpone cheese, egg whites, sugar, and marsala wine. The biscuits are sprinkled with strong coffee and the marsala, and then embedded in a thick rich custard. Sometimes chocolate is also used, but that is not traditional
Topiaries - designating or of the art of trimming and training shrubs or trees into unusual, ornamental shapes
Tweed - a wool fabric with a rough surface, in any of various twill weaves of two or more colors or shades

U

Unethical – immoral, dishonest or wrong

V

Veranda - an open porch along the outside of a building
Verbiage - the manner in which something is expressed in words
Viscount - a peer who ranks below an earl and above a baron

W

Waylay - to intercept (someone) unexpectedly
Wisteria - twining woody vines or shrubs of the pea family, with fruits that are pods and showy clusters of bluish, white, pink, or purplish flowers

***Resourced from:**

- Websters-online-dictionary.org
- Yourdictionary.com
- Thefreedictionary.com
- http://soil.gsfc.nasa.gov/soil_pH/plant_pH.htm
- Encarta.msn.com
- Answers.com
- Babylon.com
- About.com

CPSIA information can be obtained at www.ICGtesting.com
264585BV00001B/55/P
9 781440 101939